In the Midst of a Raging Storm

by

Josie Allen

authorHOUSE™

1663 LIBERTY DRIVE, SUITE 200
BLOOMINGTON, INDIANA 47403
(800) 839-8640
WWW.AUTHORHOUSE.COM

First published by AuthorHouse 12/21/04

ISBN: 1-4208-0992-X (sc)

Printed in the United States of America
Bloomington, Indiana

This book is printed on acid-free paper.

Table of Contents

Chapter 1

Denise

As Denise looked over the lawn and onto the lake, she noticed the sun shining ever so brightly onto the water. The ducks were swimming in circles and it was such a glorious day. "Denise! Denise! Girl, stop daydreaming and get your butt down here and clean up this kitchen." Denise's thoughts were interrupted by her mothers yelling as she quickly responded. "Yes maam, I'm coming." As she woke up from her dream she said to herself. "This is my reality, a two-story shack with two bedrooms, and dirt out front for the lawn. You can forget the lake, we do have a neighborhood pool but my mother said the kids are nasty so we aren't allowed to get in it. I hate washing dishes but since I am the oldest I always get stuck with all the household chores. My mother works two shifts at the hospital cleaning rooms just so we can pay our rent. I have to be here for my brother and little sister because they need me." As Denise walked into the kitchen she already knew her mother probably had a long list of assignments for her to do.

"Denise, I have to get ready for work so I want you to wash Jeanine's hair and plait it for me. Then lay the kids clothes out for school tomorrow." "Yes maam." "Make sure that you all have finished your homework before you go to bed tonight. Now I have to go so I will see you in the morning." As Denise watched her mother, Ms. Nina Combs, walk down the street to get on the bus she noticed what a beautiful woman she was. Jeffrey and Jeanine gave her a big hug and said, "We don't know what we would do without you, sis." "Oh yeah, well I know one thing you better get going on your homework because I will be checking it."

When they both dashed into the bedroom, Denise realized she had a book report due so she pulled out her book bag and started writing. By the time they had finished their homework it was seven o'clock so she started to wash Jeanine's hair and she turned on the cartoons for Jeffrey. Denise felt like she had twins, instead of two siblings. Being a senior in high school wasn't easy, not to mention the fact that she could never partake in any of the after school programs because she had to watch her brother and sister. Denise really hated her mother for putting this burden on her and never even considering her feelings. She would never blame Jeanine or Jeffrey because she thought they were the best kids anyone could ask for and she just loved them to death. But sometimes she just wanted to hang out with her friends or act like a teenager for once. She knew she could never explain this to her mother because she would have slapped her silly if Denise even looked like she was going to talk back to her. On the other hand her sister and brother didn't really pay Nina much attention, they acted like Denise was their mother and she was just someone who paid their rent. Actually it did seem that way, so Denise couldn't blame them. She wished she was in a different place and time and her life was totally different. Denise uttered to herself, "I hate my mother, I hate this house, and I hate being Denise!" After finishing Jeanine's hair they all went to bed so that they could get up the next morning for school.

"Wake Up! Wake Up! This is WKUZ and it is time to Wake UP America!" Denise jumped up and turned off her alarm to get ready for school. She went to the library first to type up her book report before first period. Over the years she had become a really good typist, so it didn't take her long. As she looked up at the clock she noticed she had ten minutes until first period as she typed her last sentence. "Man... I am

4

done in the nick of time." As Denise stretched her hands out, she could feel someone standing behind her. "Hey my beautiful black sister." "Hey Todd, how are you?" Todd was a super fine honey, but none of the girls at school gave him the time of day. Although it could have been that Todd didn't pay them any attention because his focus was on God and his school work. As he looked down at Denise he smiled and said, "I am highly favored in the Lord." "You are what! Oh no, here we go again. Why is it every time I see you, you are preaching the Jesus to somebody, what's up with that?" "Well my sister, it is preaching the gospel. I am one of God's servants and it is my duty to reach out to my brothers and sisters and inform them of the Joy of Jesus Christ." "Yeah…Yeah, whatever you say. Look later for all that, I have to get to class." "Oh, Denise my church is having Revival next week. Would you like to be my guest?" "Church, Ha…hah. Church! Me! At church… you're joking right." "Ah…No sister Denise I am not joking I think you would find it very inspiring." "Look Todd, I am a virgin and whatever ploy you are trying to pull to get into my pants won't work." "Denise I can't believe you think I am like these thugs out here.

First of all I am also a virgin and don't plan to do anything with anybody until I am married. Secondly I would never use my Father to get next to anyone for my own pleasures." Todd took his commitment to God very seriously and his feelings were hurt that Denise would think he had other intentions. Todd walked away and said, "I'll see you later Denise." "I feel like such a fool. I can't believe I said that to Todd. I should have known he is too much into that God stuff to try a stunt like that, but he just gets on my nerves with that Bible stuff all the time. Oh well he'll get over it."

Denise hurried to get to her class. She had hoped she would have time to go by Joe's locker. Denise and Joe had been talking about being together for a few weeks now, but she was a little apprehensive about being his girlfriend. She knew that he had a bad reputation of being a bad boy and a womanizer, but he swore to her he had changed his ways. He made her feel very special and she loved to be with him. She knew her mother wouldn't approve so she didn't see him outside of school. As she approached her first period class, Joe walked up behind her and hugged her around the waist. "Hey baby! You sure are looking good today." "You are looking mighty fine yourself." "Look I have to get to class, but I will see you at lunch okay." "That's cool." "Today I am walking my girl home." "I don't know Joe, besides I haven't agreed to be your girl." "Well you will and I am walking you home." As Joe ran down the hallway she knew she couldn't resist him and he wasn't about to let her.

Chapter 2

Nina

As Nina walked up the steps to her house she could barely get the key in the door from being so tired. "I am exhausted, working these two shifts have burned me out. I still don't have enough money to pay the rent. I better call Mr. Fred and let him know I'm going to be late again." Suddenly there are loud knocks at the door which startle Nina. (Bang… Bang… Bang…) "Now who could be knocking on my door like that this time of morning, who is it?" Nina looked through the peephole and saw that it was Mr. Fred. She really was not in the mood to make up a story about why she was going to be late on her rent again. She just wanted to take a nap. It was obvious he wasn't going away so she opened the door for him. "Hey Freddy how are you?" "Save it Nina, where is my rent?" "Ah…look here, I'm running a little low on my rent money. See the thing is I had some unexpected bills this month and now I don't have enough for my rent. Can you cut me a break? You know I'm good for it." "Well Nina, you know I got overhead and folks I got to answer too. I can't keep cutting you slack. Now the only reason I did it for you last month was because I know you by yourself and you got them three kids to take care of. I know being a single mother aien't easy but I got a business to run. Now what you gonna give me for letting you slide again?" Nina knew what Freddy wanted. She knew that Freddy was in love with her, but he was not her type. Freddy was just an average looking guy who was overweight. But Nina was a hot bombshell that did not go for average. In fact she was so critical that she didn't think any man could match her standards. Deep down inside she used that for an excuse because she was simply tired of dealing with dead end relationships and tired men.

She had enticed Freddy before to get out of paying her rent and she was surprised that she actually enjoyed it. Every now and then she didn't mind Freddy coming around, but by no means was she going to make him a permanent thing. Nina could tell Freddy was in love with her by the way he acted when they were together and she knew this time was no different. She slowly began to let go of her inhibitions about him and turned on her charm. Nina grabbed Freddy by the hand and said, "What you want, now come on Freddy. Come on Daddy you know Nina gonna take care of you. You can do me this one itty bitty favor. You got plenty of properties. Now I know this one little two story house aien't gonna set you back by much. Besides… aren't you a high roller Daddy. You know I think you look real fine in that big Cadillac you drive." Freddy wanted to be with Nina so bad, but he knew her beauty was way out of his league. He was satisfied to have her in any way he could get her. He started to get excited about just the thought of being with her one more time. He blushed at the thought of her thinking about him riding in his Cadillac as he said, "Oh yeah, you think so well I been thinking about getting me one of those Cadillac Escalades." "Oh really, I like those, so what you want all the women now, huh." "Well you know me I'm all about getting paid, so like I said I need my rent money now." "I know what you want, it's me isn't it?" "Well you are fine and you are quite sexy." "Well I know that, so let me show you how I feel." After Nina took Freddy's hand and led him into my bedroom she knew she didn't have to worry about the rent money, at least not for this month.

After Freddy left she decided to take a nap, as Nina was lying in the bed she felt like she was a cheap prostitute. "I told myself after the last time with Freddy that I would never put myself in this position again. I know I need to do better and be a better mother for my kids but I really don't know how. I feel like I am just going through the motions from day to day and watching my own daughter raise my younger kids better than I can. I feel like such a failure and every time I try to do right, something comes along to knock me back down. First it was Denise's father, who ran off and left me when she was a month old. He said he wasn't ready to be a daddy. The child support that he sends is barely enough to cover one utility bill a month. He never even made an attempt to come and see her or ask about her. Then several years later I thought I would marry the twin's father, but that didn't work out either. He ended up sleeping with every woman in town and to say the least he wasn't even tactful about it. Eventually he had messed with the wrong woman and her husband ended up killing him after catching them together. The only thing I could tell the twins was that their father was in a better place. Luckily they never knew him anyway. I know I am a stubborn girl, but I am determined to make it on my own somehow, I just need to think of a way to bring in some extra money. Maybe I should ask Denise to watch other kids in the neighborhood to bring in some extra money. I will talk to her about it tonight, but for now I need to get to some rest."

As Nina finally fell asleep she could hear the twins coming in the door from school. "Stop pulling my hair!" "No, you stop stepping on my feet." "I'm a tell mama you keep messing with me." "Go ahead mama's girl." "I am not a mama's girl, big head." She jumped up from her sleep as she heard the twins in one of their debates. "I should've known I wouldn't be able to get any sleep around this house." As the twins were fussing at each other Nina jumped between them. "Okay you two enough is enough I am trying to sleep in here, quiet down." Nina looked around wondering why Denise hadn't come in from school with them. "Where is Denise?"

Jeanine looked up at her with an innocent face and said, "She's outside talking to some boy." "She's where, doing what! Nina ran to the front door in her silk blue bathrobe yelling through the screen door, "Denise! Denise! Get your butt in this house." Denise couldn't believe her mother was at the front door yelling in her night clothes. She was so embarrassed that she wanted to turn around and run. But she knew if she did her mother would come running after her, which would make her feel even worst. She decided to hurry and get in the house before her mother caused her anymore embarrassment. She looked at Joe and she could tell he was very irritated and so was she. "Dag, she gets on my nerves. Look Joe I have to go, I'll see you tomorrow though right?" Joe was sick of Denise's mother treating her like a third grader and he was ready to forget about even pursuing a relationship with her, so he just brushed her off and said, "Yeah you'll see me, bye."

As Denise strolled into the house, Nina was outraged at her daughter's behavior. "What is your fast behind doing out there talking to some boy?" Nina knew her daughter was not fast, but she was upset and the words just seemed to roll off her tongue. "First of all mama, I am not fast and I am almost out of high school. Joe is the first boy that I seem to like and you have to go and embarrass me like that. I mean was it necessary for you to yell to the top of your lungs my name, like I am some three year old child outside by herself. When am I going to be able to be a teenager, enjoy my life, what about go on a date? Huh, mama! When can I go to a school dance or hang out with my friends? It's not fair." (Denise began to cry uncontrollably) Nina could see her daughter's pain and she thought about what she said. Her daughter was right, she should be able to hang out with her friends and do normal things that the other seniors were doing. She knew that Jeanine and Jeffrey were not Denise's responsibility, but her own. She also felt guilty for giving Denise so much responsibility, but she really had no choice. "Look baby you're right and I'm sorry. I have been so busy running around here trying to keep food on the table and a place for us to stay that I have lost sight of what is really important." Denise couldn't believe her mother was taking her side. But she wasn't going to let her get off that easy. "Oh yeah and what is important to you mama?" "Well of course my three babies. I promise you baby, mama is going to start doing better and letting you do stuff with your friends. I know it's not fair honey, but I really don't have anyone else to watch Jeffrey and Jeanine. Besides I can't afford a babysitter right now.

But we will try to work something out okay, is that fair enough?" Denise was so excited that her mother took her feelings into consideration for once, so she was willing to compromise. "Yes that's fair and I didn't mean to talk back to you mama, I'm sorry. It's just that I see my friends doing all this cool stuff and going places and when they ask if I can go I always have to say no, even though I want to go." Nina wanted to allow Denise to do something special for herself for a change. She thought it was the least she could do for her daughter after all her daughter did for her. "Okay, now tell me what is the next thing happening at school that you want to go to." "Well there is a high school dance coming up next week and Joe asked if I would go with him, but I told him I couldn't. Mama, can I go... please!" Nina was excited about Denise being able to go to a dance. She thought that would be the perfect outing for Denise to make her feel special. Even though she didn't always show it, she loved Denise with all her heart. "Okay you got it, you can go. I will put in a leave slip for that night off, but I want to meet this boy before you go anywhere with him." "Yes maam!!" Denise was glowing all over and jumping around from excitement, she couldn't wait to tell Joe. She ran up the stairs saying, "I'll call him now to let him know!" Nina just laughed at her daughter's excitement and was glad that she could do something to make her happy. "Yeah okay, whatever Miss Girl, but don't get too comfortable."

Nina knew how Denise felt because she was brought up raising her own siblings and it wasn't fair. She also knew that it was her only choice at this point, but she was going to make a more conscious effort to let Denise participate in school activities.

Chapter 3

Things Aren't Always as They Seem

Denise had Joe's number on speed dial as she hit the button she tried to catch her breath. "Hello, can I speak to Joe?" "Yeah this me, who is this?" "It's me silly, Denise." "Whaaat! Your mom's actually let you make a phone call." "Yeah whatever, anyway she said I can go to the dance with you next week, isn't that great?" Joe was shocked that Denise's mother was letting her go to the dance. He was actually banking on her not being able to go because he had other plans. "Well I hate to tell you this but, it would have been greater last week but I already have a date. I mean... I wasn't going to miss the coolest dance of the year just because your mom's is trippin." Joe knew how insensitive he sounded, but he didn't care. If Denise planned on being with him she had to know that he called the shots.

Denise couldn't believe her ears; she sat there in shock with her mouth wide open. "What do you mean you already have a date, who is it?" "Now see there you go, trippin!" Silent tears began to flow down Denise's cheeks as her heart ached and she became furious. "Joe! I want to know what girl is going to the dance with my man?" "Hold up baby, I'm a lover not a fighter. I don't want no turmoil. I asked Claire, but it's just a dance. Plus you said you didn't think you could have a boyfriend because your mom's always got you tied down with your sister and brother. So how did I become your man all of a sudden?" Denise had kind of decided on her own that Joe was going to be her man because she liked him and he really seemed to be interested in her. Then she realized after what he said that she felt like a fool.

"Well I thought…I mean I like you and I thought you liked me. Oh just forget it! Have fun at your dance!" Denise slammed the phone down (Click!) and cried herself to sleep.

The next morning as she arrived in school she was in a daze trying to look for books in her locker. She noticed Todd walking towards her from the other end of the hallway. "Hey Denise, how is it going?" "Oh, hey Todd." "You seem a little down is everything okay?" Todd was always a good listener and Denise felt like she really needed to talk to someone right now. "Do you ever feel like your world is just falling apart and there is no where to turn and there is no one waiting in the wings to listen?" "Well I use to feel like that until I found my comfort in the Lord. You see knowing that my Father is always by my side and on my side is all that I need to survive. No man or woman can replace his love. Deuteronomy 7:9 states… know therefore that the Lord your God is God: he is the faithful God keeping his covenant of love to a thousand generations of those who love him and keep his commands. You see, Denise you have to make up in your mind that you are not going to allow your circumstance or situation to be your final destination. You have the power to change your direction. But you cannot see that without having faith. Denise, faith allows us to believe and see things that others think are impossible or out of our reach. Faith allows us to float on a cloud even when we are thrown out on the street. God has given you the vessel, now you just need to have the faith to put the vessel into motion."

Denise was always amazed at how much Todd knew about the Bible and how strong his faith was. She had never met anyone like him. He was such a strong person that it seemed like nothing ever bothered him. She also knew that she was nothing like him. She was very fragile and at times she felt like if the wind blew hard enough she would be knocked down.

Denise never explored anything that Todd said because she felt like it was false hope. "Todd all that sounds great but you don't understand. The boy I thought liked me is now taking some other girl to the dance. This is the same annual dance that I never was allowed to go too. And now this year my mother lets me go, but now I can't go because I don't have a date. I am one big joke and I just feel wiped out." Todd sympathized with Denise and he wanted to do something to make her feel better. "I tell you what, how about I take you to a dance Friday night? I guarantee it will be a night to remember and you will have the best time of your life." Denise was not sure about going to the dance with Todd. But she knew she did not want to miss this opportunity to get out of the house. Then she started to think she could get to the dance to see Joe and make him jealous, so she agreed to go. "Well I don't know…I guess so. I know I am not going to give up the only night I get to go out. So okay, I'm game." "Great, I'll pick you up at 7pm." "Cool, see you then. Oh, Todd thanks for the sermon but can you leave all that preaching at home Friday night? I just want to have fun." Todd just smiled and walked away as he headed towards his first class.

The school bell starts to ring (Ring! Ring!) Denise didn't realize it was time for class already and her first period teacher did not play when it came to students being late for class. "Oh shoot there's the first period bell I better get to class." Denise races down the hallway and slides into her seat, as she opens up her purse to get a tissue she notices her friend Tina. "Whew!! I just made it." Tina turns around to greet her friend. "What's up girlfriend?" "Hey Tina girl, what's up with you?" "Nothing much, so is the warden going to let you go to the dance or what?"

"Girl let me tell you what happened, mom's said I could go and do you know that no good snake is taking that all around the way girl Claire." "Stop playin…are you for real? Girl you want me to beat her down for you?" "No, I aien't trippin, she can have him. I'm going to the dance with Todd." "Todd who? Hold up… Hold up… Don't tell me you are going with Bible Boy. Girl, are you crazy? I mean Bible Boy is fine but he is too much into that God, Jesus stuff for me." "Yeah, I know but it's not like that. I just look at him as a friend and I already know everybody is going to be at the dance with a date. So I just want to go…okay. Plus I am going to wear this drop dead gorgeous dress and make Joe eat his heart out." "Oh I got you! Okay now I get it. So you just using Todd to get to the dance but then when you get there you gonna step on old girls toes for taking your man, right?" "Yeah and you know this man!!" "That's my girl."

A whole week had gone by and Denise had been on pins and needles about the dance. She was so excited that tonight was finally the night that she would get to show Joe what he was missing out on. She knew when she walked into the room with this dress he would drop Claire like a bad habit. Denise was standing in front of the mirror trying to get ready for her date for the dance. Denise always talked to herself in the mirror when she was nervous, "It's Friday night and I am making sure I look extra pretty. I am going to have Joe eating out of my hands. This pink dress hugs all my curves and I know I look good." Denise's mother walks in her room and notices just how beautiful her daughter is. "Oh Denise you look absolutely stunning."

"Thanks mom, would you help me with my zipper?" "Sure, turn around I have something for you." Nina places a pearl necklace around her daughter's neck. As the pearls fall around Denise's neck she is in awe of the rich and smooth texture that they have. "Wow! Mom this necklace is gorgeous, but it looks expensive." "Well baby girl, it is expensive. It was your grandma's. I know I don't let you do a lot of stuff and I know that you are growing up. Well I just want tonight to be special for you because you deserve it." "Dag…mom you're going to make me cry." "No don't do that because then your makeup will run." As they both laughed they were interrupted by knocking at the front door. (Knock! Knock!) "Oh my goodness that must be Todd, I have to hurry." "I thought his name was Joe?" Denise neglected to tell her mother that Joe had dumped her and she had a new date. Now she really didn't have time to get into all of that because he was already at the door. "Quick note ma, Joe dumped me so now I'm going out with Todd. But Todd is strictly a friend so it's just like two girls hanging out so now you have nothing to worry about. So hurry and get the door before my friend leaves." Nina didn't want to spoil her daughter's night so she just went along with it and answered the door.

"Good afternoon Ms. Combs, my name is Todd and I'm here to pick up your daughter." "Yes, come on in Todd." Denise did not want her mother giving Todd a lecture so she rushed to get him out the door. As she ran past her mother and took Todd's hand she said, "Okay I'm ready let's go." Todd didn't know why Denise was in such a rush so he politely waved goodbye to Ms. Combs as he was hurled out to his car. "Have a Good Evening Ms. Combs, I promise I'll have her home early."

"Okay have fun." Once they got in the car, Todd noticed how pretty Denise looked all dressed up. "Denise you look beautiful." "Thanks Todd, you look nice too." Todd pulled out onto the street and started to head toward the parkway. He knew Denise had asked him not to talk about church, so he was trying to respect her request for now. He decided to turn the radio on to a mellow jazz station.

Denise couldn't wait to get to the school she wasn't really interested in small talk with Todd, so she just remained quiet and sunk into her own thoughts. She started to think as she was riding down the street how wrong it was that she was using Todd just to get back at Joe. But then she thought she couldn't worry about that she was on a mission and her feelings were not to be played with. After riding for fifteen minutes, Denise thought they should have been to the school by now. She started to look around and noticed that her surroundings did not look familiar. "Hey Todd, where are you going the school is back that way?" "Yeah I know where the school is but that isn't where our date is." At that moment Denise was furious. "What!" Todd knew she wouldn't go along with his idea, so he just decided to make her go for it. He knew it was wrong, but he wanted to see if he could show her something new in her life that would help her. "Can you be a little open minded for one night? I would like to show you something." Denise was not in the mood for a detour with Todd, but she knew at this point she had no other choice. "Okay but make it quick, we are going to miss all the good jams. You know the DJ is like that and I know the light show is going to be off the hook."

Todd pulls the car into a parking lot. "Why are we parking here? Hold It! Hold It! Can you please explain to me why you have parked this car in front of a church?" "Well when I asked you out I told you I was going to take you to a dance, I never said the school dance. This is my church and we are having revival tonight. We are also having a gospel concert and some very interesting key note speakers. I guarantee you the Holy Ghost party is live up in here." "Look Mr. Todd! I demand that you take me to the dance and take me now." "Just come in with me and check it out. If you don't like it after thirty minutes I will take you to your dance." "Thirty minutes! And I mean thirty minutes, not a second longer…let's go!" When Denise walked in the church she was in awe at its beauty. The atmosphere was dim and there were shimmering lights all over. The place was decorated in purple and gold and everything looked so lavish and plush. Then she opened her ears to the most beautiful sound she had ever heard. The choir was singing about Jesus, and they were in perfect harmony. Denise followed Todd to a seat near the front and sat down. She didn't want him to know she was impressed so she kept a tight face and he just looked at her and smiled. Then a heavy set woman came from behind the curtain singing about the Lord being her salvation and sister girl could blow. Denise didn't know why, but that song made her cry. Then Todd looked over at her and held her hand as he asked her if she wanted to leave. But she couldn't…Denise didn't want too…and something inside her wouldn't let her. So she told him no, she was fine.

Then the woman next to Denise gave her a tissue and said, "Isn't Sister Tonya a blessing to us, she always makes me cry too. When I think about how good the Lord has been to me…when I start to think about his mercy…AHHH Lord… Help me Lord!!" Then Denise looked at her and the woman was jumping and shouting and screaming "Jesus! Jesus! Jesus!" And that made her cry even harder. She could feel Todd squeezing her hand and rubbing it. After the service, Todd went up to the Pastor and motioned Denise to come along. So reluctantly she followed him. Todd was very confident as he walked up and shook the Pastor's hand. "Hi Pastor, that was an awesome sermon you delivered I was truly blessed by it." "Thank you son and who is this new lovely Child of God I see before me?" "This is my class mate and friend Denise. Instead of going to our high school dance I decided to bring her to the Word of God." "Todd I wish more of our youth were like you son. Well Denise, welcome to our congregation. We are all family here and if you ever need anything we are here to help. We have all sorts of youth ministries and I know Todd has told you all about them because he heads most of them up." Denise was impressed with Todd's accomplishments in the church and how pleased the Pastor was with him. "Well uh no, he hasn't really. I am not really into a church right now." "Oh I see, well I hope our service has touched your heart." Denise felt uncomfortable talking to the Pastor. She had never spoken directly to a preacher before and she felt like he could see right through her. "Yes sir…I mean yes Pastor it has, thanks." Todd could sense that Denise was uncomfortable and he did not want to make her feel that way; that was never his intentions.

In fact he had hoped she would feel so comfortable that she would want to keep coming back. "Well Pastor I'll see you tomorrow I have to get her home." "Okay good night kids, God bless you." Once they were seated in the car, Todd wanted to make sure Denise was okay with how the evening went. "So…I know it was a bit much for you because it was your first time here, but Revival is always high in the spirit. But then again so is our regular service. Anyway, how did you like it, and be honest with me?" Denise was surprised that she actually enjoyed it. "Well honestly

Todd when you first brought me here I was angry with you. After I listened and watched the service I really got into it. I was surprised at how moved I was by the service and I can't believe I actually cried. I enjoyed it and I can't believe I'm saying this, but I would like to come back sometimes with you. I mean if that's okay with you, I don't want to embarrass you or anything." "Of course you can come back with me. Embarrass me, you could never embarrass me. Denise I think you are one of the most intelligent and beautiful girls I have ever met. I would be truly honored if you would attend service with me."

"Todd, that is sweet of you to say. I just meant that I don't know much about God and reading the Bible. My mama just never had the time to take us to church so I guess what I'm saying is, I don't know how to act like church folks." "I think you did just fine tonight. God accepts us just as we are, and I think that you were perfectly made in his sight." "You know what Todd…you are not like anybody I have ever met." "I know." Todd pulled into the front of Denise's house and got out to walk her to the front door and said, "Good night."

As Denise walked through the front door she tried to be very quiet so she wouldn't wake everyone up. As she walked towards the stairs she noticed the TV was on in the living room and then her mom walked up behind her and stood right in her face. "So, how was the dance? That boy Todd was cute. He didn't try anything did he? Did you kiss him?" "Mom, slow down! I told you, me and Todd are just buddies so of course I didn't kiss him. The dance was boring." "What about Joe, was he there?" "I don't know…I didn't see him. I'm tired, I'm going to bed." "Okay baby…I'm going to finish watching my movie and then I'll be up in a minute."

Denise didn't know why she lied to her mom about the dance. She just didn't feel like explaining to her how they ended up in church. As soon as she got into her pajama's the phone started to ring. (Ring! Ring!) Before Denise could get to it, her mother had picked it up and was yelling upstairs, "Denise, telephone." "Who could be calling me this late?"

"Hey Denise, its Joe." "What do you want and why are you calling me? I thought you would still be out licking up behind Claire like the dog you are." "First of all baby I was wrong. I was mad that you couldn't go with me so I asked Claire to go. So when you told me you could go, I still had to hold my ground to show you I was mad. That was my fault for playing games with you. You know I love you. It's just hard for me to get close to you because your mom's is always blocking our time." "So what happened with you and her anyway?" "I took her to the dance and when I saw that you weren't coming we left early and I took her home. Nothing happened she just isn't the girl for me. You are my girl, right baby?"

"I don't know Joe, you really hurt my feelings." "How can I make it up to you? Denise when I am around you I feel so good. Please don't leave me now, I was wrong and I let my big ego get in the way of how I really feel about you. Come on, give me another chance." Denise was glad that Joe had decided to take her back. She thought he was the cutest boy in school and she was proud to be on his arm. She wasn't about to let Claire steal her man that easy, so she agreed to forgive him. "Okay I guess so." "Thank you baby, but I need you to promise me something if we are going to be together again, can you do that?" "Yeah, what is it?" "First do you love me?" "Yes!" "Are you my girlfriend?" "Yes!" "Will you make more time for me when I need you?" "Well, yes I'll try, but…" "No, Denise! No excuses will you make time for me?" "Okay, yes I will!" "Will you start to let me do more than just hold your hand?" "Do more like what?" "You know…like maybe kiss you." "I don't know Joe that is going a little far." Denise wanted to be Joe's girl, but she didn't want to be forced into doing anything she didn't want to do. She also knew if she didn't agree to it, he would probably be kissing on some other girl. Besides she could kiss him and still keep her virginity. Joe was becoming impatient with Denise's good girl attitude. "Denise will you or won't you! Look this is what I need from my girlfriend, so are you with me or not?" "Okay Joe, yes I will kiss you." "That's my girl, I'll call you tomorrow. I love you." "I love you too, Joe."

Chapter 4

Todd

As Todd got down on his knees this morning, he felt like his spirit was going to burst out of his chest. It was such a blessing to have Denise by his side in church but he wanted to be sure that he did not allow his manly flesh to take any part in her search for God. "Dear heavenly Father, I come before you today with worship in my heart and your wonderful presence on my mind. I need you always Lord. I bless your name Father for waking me up this morning. I thank you for providing our family with shelter and food and God you just keep making a way for us to continue to be blessed. Dear Lord I know you were shining your light on Denise at church the other night and I know your hand is upon her life even though she doesn't know it. Lord I just ask you to bless her and her family. Help her mother to be the best that she can be and help Denise see that she is capable of having and doing anything in life, Lord. It all belongs to you anyway Father! I know that I am starting to develop feelings for her. Lord I ask that you give me the strength to discern from my fleshly feelings and continue to focus on saving another soul for the kingdom. Lord I love you, I worship you...I adore your holy name!! It is in the name of Jesus Christ I pray. Amen and Amen!"

As Todd began to get up from his morning praise he heard his mother calling him, "Todd! Todd! Breakfast is ready baby." "Okay mom I'm coming now." "Good morning baby." Todd's mother always greeted him with a kiss on the cheek. (Kiss) "Good morning mom, how did you sleep?" "Just like a baby. I got up at 5am and had my private time with the Lord just like I like it before dawn and then I decided to make you this big breakfast because I knew my growing boy was going to get up hungry." "Well you're right about that, I am starving. It looks great, thanks Ma."

"You know I am waiting to hear about your date that you took to church." "Mom, it was not a date. We are just two friends and that's it. I know she is going through a lot right now so I thought Revival might uplift her spirit."

"Well aren't you just being Mr. Secretive." "No, really there is nothing to tell. I took her to Revival, she said she enjoyed it and asked if she could come again sometime, that was it." "You like her don't you?" "You know me like a book, don't you?" "You're my son aren't you?" "Okay, yes I like her. Okay, I like her a lot. I just don't think she is the woman for me though. If I can save her soul then I feel like our relationship has served its purpose whether her and I get into a relationship or not." "Well son I think that's all you can do." "God has designed the perfect woman for you and when she comes along you will know she is the one." "You're right as usual. I love you and I have to get to school." "Okay baby, have a blessed day." "Hold it come here." Todd already knew what his mom wanted and even though he would rush her along as she did this daily routine, he was thankful that she did it. "Dear Lord keep my baby covered in the blood of Jesus Christ today, no weapon that is formed against him shall prosper. Amen!" "Amen, mama." "Now I have to go, I'll see you tonight after Youth Bible study."

Todd raced to his car and turned on the gospel station on the way to school. He started to remember his father as he was driving down the rode. He remembered he was such a noble man and had served as a deacon in his church ever since Todd could remember. One night he was coming home late after one of his Feed the Homeless Ministry meetings and was struck by a drunk driver.

32

When Todd's mother received the news she was devastated, Todd was only twelve years old and he was very close to his father. Even though Todd's father was very active in the church he also owned his own Plumbing Company. He always made time for Todd and his wife. He put God and his family first in everything he did. Todd's father always told him to remember that when everything you think is important has been taken away from you, God is always there. He always told Todd to put God first, your wife second, and your children third. Everything else is just material so be thankful about what God gives you and when it is taken away bless the Lord at all times, because he knows what he is doing. They would always have talks like that about life, God, and his future. The one thing Todd and his mom didn't know was just how much his father was about his own business as well. He had Todd and his mother set up for life. He had a four million dollar life insurance policy set up for each of them. Their house was paid for and they both had brand new cars. They really didn't need or want for anything. The business now belonged to Todd's mother and it was very successful, but she decided to let her husband's brother run the daily operations and she just overlooked the books.

Todd's mother spent her time volunteering at the church and other committee's, attending social events, or just relaxing at home. Even though they were millionaires no one knew it. They kept their business very private and devoted a lot of their money to the church and needy charities, but most of it was just sitting in the bank. His mom had already put aside enough money for him to go to college and do whatever he wanted to do or have. She had also made some very strong and lucrative investments for both of them.

Instead of buying some expensive fancy BMW or Mercedes, Todd just got a brand new Nissan Sentra. He didn't want to be looked at as the rich kid and he knew that God would direct them on how he wanted them to manage and handle the money anyway. It had been six years since his father's death and it still felt like there was a lump in his throat. When Todd arrived at school he parked his car in the back parking lot and then he opened the trunk to get his book bag. As his back was turned he could feel someone walking up behind him. "Hey Todd." "Oh…hey Tina." Todd didn't really care for Tina because he knew she gossiped too much. Tina didn't care for Todd's good boy attitude, but she wanted to get the scoop of what was really going on with him and Denise. "So I heard that you and Denise went out on a date." "Oh you did, did you?" "Well yeah I did, so what's up with that?" "Look Tina, I'm late for class so I have to go." "Oh so you just going to carry me like that. Yeah okay Bible boy, that's cool and all but you know my girl is back with Joe, so you might as well save your energy." As Todd walked up the steps to the school his skin started to boil. He didn't even care that half the school nick named him Bible Boy. Being made fun of for knowing God's word was only a confirmation to him that he was a threat to the enemy so that didn't bother him in the least, but Denise going back to that two timing loser just made him angry. He raced through the busy hallways and got to his first class early just so he could collect his thoughts and calm down.

As Todd sat down, Ralph came in behind him and sat next to him. "Hey Man." "Hey Ralph, how's it going man." "I'm cool, but you look like you could hurt somebody." "Who, me? No I'm cool, I just got some disturbing news." "Anything I can do for you man." "Ah, naw I said I'm cool. It's nothing like that, I'll get over it." "Oh I get it…it must be a girl involved. I didn't think you messed with any of the girls around here. You know none of them are saved and if they are they must be hiding in a closet somewhere. I thought you were looking for the Virgin Mary, man. But hey, do your thing I think virgins are cool. You know I don't knock you man." "Ralph, it's nothing like that, just let it go." "Alright man you got it. Here comes Mr. Greer, I bet he is going to pull out a pop quiz on us today."

After a long day, school was finally over and Todd couldn't wait to get to bible study. He knew that once he got into the Word of God his spirit would calm down. As he walked towards his car, Todd felt someone tap him on the shoulder and he turned around. "Todd I'm sorry." "Hey Denise…what do you mean you're sorry, sorry for what?" "Tina told me what she said to you this morning and she had no right to make those comments. I chewed her out about it and I hope she didn't offend you." "No she didn't offend me, but she did inform me that you are going out with Joe again, is this true?" "Yes, yes it is true. It's complicated you wouldn't understand. I do like you Todd but as a friend. You and I are from two different worlds. You could never love me. Joe understands me and my situation and we can relate to each other." "I'm happy for you. If Joe makes you happy then that's great.

I just want you to know that I will always be here for you as a friend and just because you are Joe's girlfriend that doesn't mean that you can't go to church with me sometimes." "I may take you up on that offer someday." "Well it is an open invitation for life." "Todd, you are a handsome, smart, and sincere guy. I know you will make some other girl very happy to be by your side." "So if I'm all that, what is Joe to you?" "He's a handsome guy who is a bad boy adventurous type. I guess that just appeals to me."

"Well I tell you what, keep your eyes and your ears open because nothing is as it appears and guard your heart. Good luck to you Denise, I'll see you later."

When Todd got to his car he felt like he could have cried but he didn't. It wasn't because Denise did not want to be with him. It was because Todd knew what type of guy Joe was and he knew he was going to mess up her life for sure. All he could do was pray for her at this point. After bible study Todd went on his evening run with a few buddies from class. He ran four days a week for three miles each day, but on bible study night him and two other guys would run for four miles together. Todd loved running because he could let his self be free and it gave him a chance to clear his head. On the nights that Todd and the guys ran they talked about everything under the sun and gave each other support and advice. They all started to stretch when Greg said, "Hey Todd you know that Lisa has her eye on you." "Man, please…you mean the pretty Lisa that sits up front in bible study class?" "Yeah, that's her." "Come on now, you know she is on fire for the Lord, she is not in class thinking about me." "Yes, she is on fire for the Lord, but she also has her eye on you." "How do you know this?"

"I heard her tell Cantrell that she would like to get to know you better and hang out with you, but she was scared to approach you. So I told her that we were going running in the park after class and I thought her and Cantrell should come by and take a walk." "You did what! You are always trying to play match maker." "Shhh…here they come." As the girls approached them, Greg turned on his charm. "Well hello sister Lisa, hello sister Cantrell what a pleasure to see you ladies again this evening."

"We thought we would take a walk in the park." "What a great idea sister Lisa."

Todd had his mind on other things and he wished Greg would stop trying to set him up with girls in their church. Todd thought that Lisa was a perfect catch, but he felt like he didn't have the time to commit to a relationship right now, especially with anyone in his church that he would see all the time. So he sarcastically looked at Greg and said, "Yeah Greg, what a great idea and a big coincidence, huh." Lisa looked at Todd and decided to make her move, "Todd can I talk to you for a moment?" "Sure sister Lisa, guys I'll be right there just keep stretching. What can I do for you sister?" "Well brother Todd I don't want to be forward and this is the reason why I haven't said anything to you after all these years, but I like you. I have watched you grow in Christ and in our church and I have always liked you. I had to make sure that your focus was really on the Lord because that is very important to me in any young man that I go out with. I see how much you love the Lord Todd and I know how devoted you are to ministry. I have watched you become a leader for all the young people in our church and I know that you would be the perfect man for me.

A man that I could get acquainted with, marry and have children with someday. I also know that you are very humble and you would have never approached me yourself because you wouldn't want our relationship to interfere with your teaching and my focus on God. But Todd I have asked God who is the man for me and he has led me to you today. If it pleases God and if it pleases you, can we be together as a couple?" Todd was shocked he had never been approached like this before. He liked the fact that Lisa was aggressive and she was going after what she wanted. "Wow that is a lot to swallow at once. Lisa I think you are a beautiful girl, but are you sure about this? I mean I would be honored to get to know you better but this is just so sudden." "I understand and I am sorry that I just sprung this on you." "No…it's okay, really. I tell you what, why don't we start to date and just hang out as friends and get to know each other better. If we like each other then we will see where it goes and if we don't then we will always be friends." "Okay that sounds fair to me." "Great! Oh…and Lisa." "Yes!" "Can I pick you up on Saturday to go to a movie?" "Yes, you most certainly can." "Okay, see you then." Lisa was blushing all over and Todd was glad he had decided to go out with her.

He figured he might as well give it a try. He ran over to his friends grinning from ear to ear as he teased them, "Alright you slackers let's get this run off the ground because you know I beat you guys every time." As they started to run Todd was thinking about Lisa and God and how his mom said he has a woman made perfectly for him. Lisa was just that. She was beautiful, athletic, smart, and first and foremost she loved the Lord.

Her parents were also very active in the church and she was about to graduate from high school as well. She attended a Christian School for Girls on the east side of town. Todd also knew that she planned on going to Divinity School once she graduated and she wanted to be a Pastor. The girl had everything he could ever ask for in a wife, but he never asked her out because he figured she didn't give boys the time of the day. Even though Todd was saved and sanctified he still liked to have a friend to take to a movie, church, or out to eat. Another reason he didn't ask her out was because his church was like one big family and he just didn't want everyone in his business. Todd thought maybe this was God's way of showing him how to let go of worrying about what other people think. He was looking forward to taking Lisa out this weekend and after he thought about it, he always liked her but he just never allowed his feelings to manifest because he felt like there was never a chance for them.

It was Saturday morning and Todd was even more excited about his afternoon date than ever, he couldn't wait. Todd was singing and dancing throughout the house when his mother walked in the front door. "Why are you floating on cloud nine this morning?" "Good morning, ma. I have a date today." "With that girl, Denise?" "No and I told you me and Denise were just friends, it's with Lisa McBride." "The Lisa McBride that goes to our church? That pretty girl that never has a hair out of place? The one that is about to go to Divinity School and is on Holy Ghost fire for the Lord?" "Yes ma, her." "Thank you Jesus! Bless the Lord! Glory, Glory! Hallelujah God!

Lord…I asked you to bring my son a God fearing wife, a wife who loved and worshipped you, a woman who knew what is was to respect your name. But Lord you done blessed me in a mighty way! Ahhh God!! Holy Ghost hold me…" Todd watched his mother jump and shout all throughout the living room as the Holy Ghost took over her spirit and he just fanned her and blessed God for his peace and mercy. Once the Holy Ghost let her go, he just shook his head. Todd finished getting dressed and went to pick up Lisa and the whole time he was driving he started to think about what an awesome mom he had. Todd's mother had bounced back after his father passed away by throwing herself into his plumbing business. She said she never wanted to be tied down by being the boss and that is why she let Todd's uncle run it. But she knew every move that company made.

She also handled all the promotions and made it the successful company that it was today. She said this was her way of keeping the memory of his father alive. Todd never wanted his mother to be lonely, so he would try to get her to date. But she always said his father was her soul mate so there was no use in her wasting time on anybody else.

She had decided that the rest of her life was meant to be devoted to helping other people and that is where she would get her fulfillment, and that is exactly what she did. Todd's mother served on every board you could think of, as well as community organizations to help people in need. She worked at many different facilities to help out whenever she could such as: battered women's support groups, single mothers groups, homeless shelters, drug addicted support groups, and many more. She was highly respected by the entire community, but her biggest fan was Todd.

Chapter 5

Joe

"Man I am so sick of these girls bugging me. Even though I tell them they just a chick on the side and I got my girl, they still keep calling me." Joe was walking around his room talking to his self because he was tired of all his old girlfriends calling him. His phone had been ringing off the hook all morning and even though he liked the attention, he didn't feel like being bothered right now. Joe's mother was also very irritated with the constant phone calls as she screamed upstairs, "Joe! Boy I said come and get this telephone before I hang up on these little girls." "Okay, ma I got it. Yeah who is this?" "It's Claire, and what are you up to?" "I'm chillin you know its Saturday, why you asking?" "I thought me and you could hang out today." "I don't know."

Joe knew that Claire was the type of girl that would give it up easy, but the problem was she was known to get around with to many of the other guys in school. He could never take her seriously or make her his special girl. Claire knew that Joe loved Denise, but she also knew that Joe was a player and she had the body and the looks to make him beg for more so she went in for the kill, "Look, I know Denise is your girl, but you know daggone well your little girl can't come out to play. What you need to do is step up to a real senior who is about to become a woman. Denise can't even go out on a date unless she brings those two little brats. Now I know you are sick of that, so come on and have some fun for a change." Even though Joe knew it was wrong, Claire was right.

He was sick of having to wait on Denise, plus she wasn't giving it up anyway. "Okay Claire so what are you up for today?" "Whatever you want, I'm game." He got to Claire's house in about forty five minutes since she lived on the other side of town and honked his horn for her to come outside. Claire was cool and her folks were big time lawyers so they were always on the go and she was an only child. As Claire walked down the driveway toward Joe's car, Joe noticed how good she looked in the tight yellow sundress she was wearing. She jumped in the car and grabbed him by the neck, "Hey baby, what's up?" As Claire grabbed Joe's neck she turned his face toward her and gave him a long kiss on the lips. (kiss) Joe thought that Claire was a little too loose sometimes and that is exactly why she could never be the type of woman he would take home to meet his folks.

"Dag, you just come out kissing me like you my girl or something. You need to slow down, girl." "Whatever, you like it. I don't care if Denise is your girl, you are my man for the day and there aien't nothing she can do about it." "I see you go after what you want." "Do you have a problem with that?" "The question is, do you?" "Nope, so let's ride up to the coast, my parents have a beach house there and it's really cool." "For real!" "Yes silly, for real so let's go!" As they drove up the coast it was an hour and thirty minutes before they got there and they were both jammin to the hip hop and reggae sounds Joe had blasting on his CD player.

"Turn here it's the first house on the left." As they approached the house Joe was amazed at how unique the architecture was. When he got up to Claire's house it was one of the biggest one's on the block.

"Man this is tight. I wish we had something like this." "My parents bought it last year and said we would all come up here on the weekends to spend time together, but they haven't even had time to do that. I guess work is always more important. But hey, who cares were here now." Claire did care, she cared very much that her parents brushed her off with

44

materialistic things and never had time for her. To numb her feelings of being rejected she tried to get affection from any source she could. That usually meant sleeping with different boys from school or anyone she might run into that showed interest in her. Most of the time she was found with some other girls man, so she didn't have many girlfriends in school. She was glad that Joe had agreed to come after her parents decided to take a week's vacation in Paris for just the two of them. She looked at Joe and started to smile as she nestled herself in his arms.

Joe was starting to feel uncomfortable so he pushed her away, "Yeah here we are, together all alone." "Would you loosen up Joe, let's just take it slow. I think my parents have some candles under the sink." Joe watched Claire pull out two vanilla scented candles and light them and then she slipped into the bathroom. When she came out she was wearing a white and pink teddy that looked like it was from Victoria's Secret. The girl looked good and he couldn't resist her. Claire walked toward Joe and straddled herself on his lap and started to kiss him gently. "Now can Denise do this for you?" "No, she can't." The more Claire kissed him the more he started to melt into her arms and take her clothes off. Then they moved to the bedroom and continued to make love.

After they made love, Claire rested her head on his chest, "Joe I know this was our first time, but do you think we could continue to see each other like this?" "What do you mean, like this?" "You know, you pick me up, we come here and have sex. Look I won't tell Denise and no one has to know." "I don't know Claire." Joe had planned on marrying Denise and he knew if she ever found out he was with Claire again she wouldn't give him the time of day. He thought one time was cool, but to make this a habit could be deadly for both of them. Claire sensed that Joe was afraid of getting caught so she tried to reassure him, "Look I don't want a boyfriend right now, but I have to admit you handle your business in the bedroom. We can be sex partners and Denise can be your good girl and everyone's happy. I don't see what's so hard about that." "Girl you know you are cold. Plus you already got me in trouble once with Denise." "I don't know why you like that girl so much. She can't do anything for you. She can barely come outside."

"You can't help who you love. But for real I am a man and I do have needs. I know that Denise is not about to give up her virginity anytime soon, so if you are cool with this then it may benefit both of us." Joe knew he was headed for trouble, but how could he pass up an offer like this. Claire was thrilled that Joe agreed to her proposition. Now she could have him whenever she wanted him. "Now that's what I'm talking about, baby." Joe knew he was dead wrong but Claire felt so right. He couldn't believe this girl was willing to be with him just to have sex, with no strings attached. This was an opportunity of a lifetime and he was not about to pass it up. "Joe let's sleep for a little while before you take me home."

As Claire nestled in Joe's arms and got comfortable he felt like he was on top of the world. After a long evening with Claire he dropped her off at home and then headed home himself. As he walked in the house he was greeted by his mother, "Joe where have you been? You got a million phone messages and I am not your secretary." "Okay, dag ma, stop sweatin me. Who called?" "Denise called…twenty times, Jeff and a few of your other knuckle head friends, Tina, Stephanie. The point is who hasn't called. You know more people then the President boy. I ought to start charging you for these calls." When Joe's mother said Denise called him several times his heart started to beat very fast. "What if someone saw me with Claire and told her, why would she call me like that unless she was upset?"

Joe darted upstairs to grab the phone to call Denise to see what was wrong. Her phone rang once and someone picked it up, "Hello." "Hi, can I speak to Denise." "Joe, is that you?" "It's me baby, what's wrong?" "Joe, where have you been? I have been calling you all day." "Oh...I huh...I was hanging out with my boys shooting hoops. I figured you would be tied up with your peoples today." "Well I wasn't and you didn't even call me." "Jeffrey and Jeanine wanted to go to the circus so I wanted us to take them." "So you were just going to volunteer me to take you, your little brother and sister to the circus, right?" "I didn't mean it that way, but I thought this would also give us some time to be together." "Denise...us means me and you, why do we have to include Jeffrey and Jeanine on every date we go on?" "I know and I'm sorry but I have to watch them on the weekends that my mother works.

You were the one that said I need to make time for you and you knew my situation when we got together so why are you acting like something has changed?" "I know nothing has changed and that is why I am frustrated with the situation." "Well I know and I am too, but I can't leave them alone they are only seven years old." "I am not suggesting you leave them alone. I'm sorry, they are good kids and I like them around but just not all the time. When we graduate from high school next month, I plan to go to college and I need a serious relationship. Can you say that you will be able to be in a serious relationship with me if you have two kids on your back?"

"Don't you think I have thought about that? Don't you think I want a better life for me? I am going to get a full time job to help my mom out so we can afford a babysitter and then I am going to go to school part time, I have dreams too. I want to go places and see things. I want to attend nursing school, so I will just go when I can around my work schedule, that's all." "You are selling yourself short by taking some local community classes. Do you realize how long it will take for you to finish nursing school like that? I am going to NYU full time, I have already been accepted Denise. I thought we could have a future together but you are going to have to decide if you are looking for a future for yourself or is your future going to be helping your mother raise her own kids?"

Denise was shocked at how blunt Joe was speaking to her. She couldn't believe he had the audacity to disrespect her mother. Whether it was true or not he had no right to say it and she was about to explode, "Don't you dare talk about my mother and what I do for her. (Denise slammed the phone down)"

"I knew I was wrong for what I said. I didn't mean to go there, but it's time for her to step up to the plate. She will be eighteen soon and at that age she should be able to make her own decisions. I think it's real messed up that I have to go to another woman to satisfy me because she can't. I'll give her some time to cool off and call her back." Denise was outraged at Joe's blatant disrespect. "I can't believe he went there about my mama. This relationship is getting out of hand and I don't have time for it, so maybe I should just tell him it's over." (The phone rings) "Hello" "Denise…baby don't hang up. I love you and I didn't mean to say anything bad about your mom. Can you accept my apology?" "Look I was just thinking about us and maybe you're right I am not ready for an adult relationship. Why don't we just call it quits." "No sweetie! You can't do this Denise I want you so bad that it hurts and that is why I get so crazy over you sometimes. I want us to be together forever."

Joe thought he loved Denise, but the problem was he really didn't know how to love and respect a woman. When he was young his father was very abusive to his mother and ran around with other women all the time. Finally Joe's mother left him and they never heard from him again. Denise loved Joe and she had hoped they would be together forever, but she knew she couldn't go on with him treating her like this. When he said he wanted to be with her forever, she began to smile and she could feel her heart beating fast. "So what are you saying, Joe?" "Will you marry me Denise?" "Are you for real?" "Yes baby when we get out of school let's get married. It's only a month away and we could just go to the justice of the peace." "Where would we live?" "I'll get a job and you'll get a job and we can get an apartment somewhere near NYU.

We can still go to school and be married." "I know that, but who said I was moving to New York?" "Denise, Philadelphia is not that far away from New York. You can still commute here to visit your family. Plus that is where your husband will be. I am already set up to go to school out there so I can't let my family down. Now you didn't answer my question. Will you marry me?" "I love you Joe but marriage is a big step." "It's a step we will take together. For better or for worse, right baby? You know I will always take care of you. I know you're not turning my proposal down are you?" "No honey I'm not, but Joe maybe I should think about it." "Denise, I am so sick of you trying to analyze everything. There is no life here for us. Are you saying you want to live in this dump of a town forever? Is that all you want out of life? I don't know about you, but I have plans baby, big plans and I want you in them. Why are you always working against me like this?" "I'm not working against you and yes I will." "Yes you will what?" "Yes Joe, yes I will marry you." "Oh baby you make me so happy, that's my girl.

As soon as we graduate we are going to get married and start looking for a place, okay baby." "Yes baby." "But let's keep this a secret because I don't want our parents to flip out before the end of the school year on us." "I agree I would rather be eighteen before I tell my mom." "Yes I agree too. Someone has an eighteenth birthday coming up, so what do you want for your birthday?" "Just you...just you, baby." "Well you stuck with me for life now. I love you Mrs. Combs-Turner." "I love you too Mr. Joe Turner."

After Joe hung up with Denise he was very excited. He always wanted to marry a good girl and Denise was it. Joe knew if he got Denise to New York and away from her family he could have more control in their relationship. He was anxious to marry her because he knew she would be devoted to him and take care of him. Plus Joe knew it would be hard going to school and trying to make ends meet and she was a survivor. As Joe sat on his bed he said, "I will keep Claire in the wings for now but I am going to have to cut her off once we graduate. No one will know where I am when I move to New York anyway so all those chicken heads are going to be out of the picture, except for my wife, Mrs. Turner. I like the sound of that."

It had been a long day so Joe decided to turn in for the night. He was laying in bed thinking about him and Denise getting married, someday having children, and being in love. He knew things would be tight when they first got to New York, but it would be much easier having two incomes while trying to go to school. Once he got to New York he would finally have Denise all to his self. He would be the first and only man she ever touched, kissed, or made love to. Joe couldn't wait for that moment when they came together as one. That would make the wait all the more worth it.

Chapter 6

The Choices We Make

"You know you will be graduating soon. What do you want to do? I mean you never talk about it with me Denise." "Mom to be honest I don't know myself. I want to go to medical school or maybe nursing school, I haven't decided." "Well why don't you apply at the hospital I work at? I could put in a good word for you. I know you would get the job." "Mama I don't want a job. I want a career and I see how they work you like a slave cleaning up behind everybody. I don't want to work for them people." "Well that same job is what keeps a roof over our head and food on the table so don't knock nothing until you walked a mile in my shoes, baby." "I know, but maybe I want to go somewhere else, somewhere away from here." "Where is that?" "Maybe...New York." "New York? Honey let me tell you one thing, New York is big and expensive and it's a fast paced city life that aien't for everybody." "What are you saying...I couldn't make it in New York?" "Well you know what they say...if you can make it there you can make it anywhere. Baby you aien't made it nowhere yet and I don't think New York is a place you want to start with.

Anyway enough about New York, can you do me a favor?" "Yes, ma what is it?" "I have a date tonight, so can you watch the kids for me?" "A date, with who?" "Well if you must know, it's Mr. Freddy." "The landlord Mr. Freddy?" "Yes the landlord. He has tickets to this play I have wanted to see, so he asked me to go. You know actually the man is a good catch. He has a five bedroom house and he owns a lot of property, plus he is a good business man." "You don't have to sell him to me...he's your date for the evening. I didn't think he was your type." "Okay so he is a little on the chubby side but he isn't bad looking in the face.

You know he has been a good friend over the years." "I wonder why?" Denise knew something funny was going on with the two of them, but she just couldn't figure out what it was. Nina looked at her daughter wondering if she knew she had slept with Freddy before, "What was that?" "Oh nothing, I said oh my...look at the time." "Yeah, well anyway I will be leaving shortly so I'll see you later on." "Okay ma, well try and have fun."

Nina continued to get ready as she thought, "I can't believe I am going out with Freddy after our few romps in the bedroom. When he came by the other night to invite me to the play he seemed so sincere. Besides I'm sick of sitting at home without a man. (Knocks at the door) That must be him here we go, hey Freddy!" "Hey, you are looking good as always, so you ready?" "Yep!" Freddy adored Nina and he wanted her to be his wife and after six long years of watching her and trying to get into her heart he had decided that he didn't want to wait any longer. As she slid onto the leather seats he reached in the back seat and pulled out a dozen white roses. "Here Nina, these are for you." "Freddy, what is this all about?" "I know over the years our encounters with each other haven't been under the best circumstances but I want things to change. The times that we were together I didn't want to leave you. Over the years I have fallen in love with you, but I know that you probably aren't physically attracted to a guy like me. The white roses represent us starting from a clean slate, a pure slate. I want you to be my woman." "Wait a minute! I went out with you tonight because I thought we were going to a show.

I didn't come out here with you to be seduced by flowers and to get into no relationship with you." "I know Nina, but just give me a chance. I can make your life so much better. You and the kids can move in my house. I have plenty of room and you don't have to work anymore. I'll take care of you and the kids. I am just tired of being alone Nina. I fell in love with you the first time we made love. Why do you think I kept coming around and asking if you were short on your rent?" "I don't know, I thought you were concerned. So basically what you're saying is…you knew I would give it up to you for a month of free rent, so you used me." "No. Nina I didn't use you. I love you and I felt like that was the only way you would let me get close to you."

"Take me home right now!" "Nina, please don't do this. I have tickets to the show and reservations to dinner at LaMorr's. Let's just have a good evening and see how things go." "LaMorr's that expensive upscale restaurant downtown?" "Yes baby that's the one. I would do anything for you Nina. If you were with me you could eat there every night if you want. I can give you anything you want Nina. But I want you, can you give me that?"

"I don't know…let's see how I feel after LaMorr's." As they drove off in Freddy's new Cadillac Escalade Nina sat back and got comfortable. She thought if she decided to be with Freddy she could stop working and finally get into a nice house. She could even have a car for a change. She thought to her self, looks aren't everything and that is probably why she didn't have a man now. So she needed to think about his proposition before she said no. When they arrived at the theatre they had the best seats in the house.

They laughed and joked as the play went on. Once Nina got to know Freddy as a person she thought he was a pretty nice guy. After the play they arrived at the restaurant around nine o'clock as they walked through the revolving door, Nina noticed the place was packed. "Mr. Townson your table is ready." Before they could get in the door the hostess was escorting them to their seats. The waiting area was full and people were looking at them wondering why they were going ahead of them.

"Can you please explain to me how you did that?" "Did what?" "How did we get to walk in front of all those people?" "I'm a regular here, plus I am one of the owners of this restaurant." "Yeah right...you own this restaurant?" "I said I was a co-owner. A few other business men and myself got in on this place with the original owner to keep it going before it became big time. Now that it is big time we are reaping all the cash benefits." "I must say, I am impressed. I never knew all this about you." "There is a time and place for everything and I am willing to share all this with you, but you will have to be committed to me."

"Freddy, let's just take things one day at a time. I have had a wonderful time tonight, but as far as me moving in with you, I don't know." "We have known each other for six years now Nina. How much longer am I going to have to wait?" "Okay, that may be true but I have only known that you wanted me to live with you for about four hours." "You're right and I can't expect your feelings to be the same as mine." They sat in silence and ate their food. The more Nina thought about it, the more she wanted to do it. She was tired of struggling and she wanted Denise to be able to go to college, she thought maybe this was God's way of opening a door for her.

After a delicious dinner, Freddy took her hand and they walked outside into the night air and there it was...just sitting there. It was a horse drawn carriage with a man waving his hands for them to come over. Freddy grabbed Nina's hand and said, "Come on!" He led her to the carriage and put his arms around her once they were seated. "Freddy you are too much for me, this is wonderful." "Where to Mr. Townson?" "Anywhere she wants to go." "I don't know where to go…huh, just drive around the block." "Yes, maam!" As the horse started to gallop around Nina looked at Freddy and he started to look better and better. He put his arms around her and she hugged him back and then they started to kiss. "Nina?" "Yes Freddy?" "I love you and I always have. You don't have to say it back if you don't mean it, but I want you and your kids to come and live with me. I can make a better home for you and you can learn to love me in due time." "Let me talk to them and I'll think about it, okay." "That's all I can ask of you."

Nina got home around midnight and she was on cloud nine. She couldn't sleep thinking about how much nicer it would be for the kids to have a home in the suburbs with a nice back yard. She wanted to be able to attend more school functions with them and take them places. She walked around the kitchen talking to her self, "Denise has to go to college, she is too smart to let all her hard work go to waste." "Mom?" "Denise, baby what are you doing up?" "I couldn't sleep so I decided to make a sandwich, do you want one?" "Oh no, we went to eat at LaMorr's." "For real, so what was it like? I heard that place was off the hook." "Well it was that and then some.

The kicker is that Freddy is a co-owner in the restaurant and we got first class service. It was like we were celebrities or something." "For real! I didn't know Mr. Freddy was rolling in the dough like that." "Yes he is! Plus I told you he has this big house in the suburbs and he owns all this other property. Did you see his new Escalade?" "He got a new Escalade, what...for real!" "Girl, stop saying for real." "Okay, ma I'm sorry but I am shocked. I didn't know he had it going on like that." "Well the man definitely has it going on as a business man." "So do you like him now?" "What kind of question is that?" "Looks aren't everything and cash goes a lot further, so do you like him?" "Yes, I think I do. Can you believe that he had a horse drawn carriage take us around the city after dinner? I have never had such a fairytale date in all my life. I want that! I want that for us! I want you to be able to go to college and see and do things that I never could do. I want Jeanine and Jeffrey to have the world and I want to be there for them more. As it stands I can't do any of that for any of you and I am tired of coming up short every month.

Not just financially short but I am falling short of being a mother and I hate myself for it. (Crying, sobbing, sniffing)" "Momma, nobody blames you for having to work all time. I know you are doing your best to raise us. Momma...please don't cry because you are going to make me cry." "I'm sorry baby, I'll stop crying." "Here's a tissue." "Thank you. Denise?" "Yes, ma." "How would you like it if we moved in with Freddy?" "You mean leave this, two bedroom duplex to move into a five bedroom mansion?" "It's a big house, but it's not a mansion, but yes that's what I mean.

Freddy asked me tonight if we would all like to come and live with him. But I would have to agree to be his girlfriend, so that means we would be a couple and possibly get married in the future. What do you think?" "It's not about what I think, what do you think?" "I think I like him and in due time I could learn to love him. What I know is that we would all have a better life and I could finally start to be a better mother to you guys."

"Then I say go for it! What do we have to loose, when can we pack?" "I didn't think you would be this gun-ho about this idea. You could have at least left me in suspense for one day." "Well, I look at it this way. There is nothing here for us. I will be going away to school and Jeffrey and Jeanine will need more of your time, so this works out great." "Hold it young lady! What do you mean you are going away to school? Have you been accepted to some college and haven't told me?" "No not exactly. I have been meaning to talk to you about this, but I was waiting for the right time. Joe asked me to marry him." "Joe did what! I am going to kill him! How dare him come up in my house and propose to my child without my consent. I don't even know this little snake. I have only met him a few times and then he didn't look like no marriage material to me. Have you slept with him?" "No ma I haven't. Joe isn't like that. He knows that I plan to stay a virgin until I get married." "Oh so that's why he pops us with this proposal, he is trying to get in your pants."

"No…you see that is why I didn't tell you because I knew you would react this way. I am going to be eighteen very soon and I can make my own decisions and I am marrying Joe and moving to New York and you can't stop me."

"You are doing what and moving where! Where is my belt! I will beat a seventeen year old child down at one o' clock in the morning. (Nina runs through the house searching for her leather belt) No stay right there, I'm going to find it! Jeffrey and Jeanine probably done hid my belt. Believe me girlfriend I will find it, now where in the world did them kids put it." "Ma! Ma! Stop it! I am not a child anymore and I don't need a spanking I need my mother to tell me I have her blessing and support." "Well I can't do that. I don't know this boy and I don't know you anymore Denise.

What has gotten into you? You used to want more out of life. You used to think about things before you did them." "I do think about things. I have thought about this for awhile and I want to go. I love him, mama. I want to marry him and I need you to say its okay. Besides, you all will be in a new house and you will have a much better life. Why can't you let me find my own way in this world?"

"Because it's not what you think it is and that boy is not about what you think he is. Denise you have to be smarter than that. Laying up with some teenage boy in New York without a job is not living…it is giving up. You are taking the easy way out of life. Do you think once you get to New York you will still get your education?" "Well yes…I mean that's the plan." "It seems to me he has made all the plans, you have just gone along with them. I beg you not to do this, you need to make your own way in life and he is not it." "Well what is life like for you? You act like we have some glamorous life, you didn't go to college." "Don't you ever question my life young lady. I have made sacrifices for you all your life and that is why I want better for you.

Don't go to New York on a pipe dream and get pregnant like I did, now where is your father? No where to be found, that's where. You deserve better than this Denise and why can't you see that for yourself?" "Mama I do see that and I am smart, but this is the way I feel right now and I have to make my own decisions and my own mistakes in life. Why can't you just let me do that?" "Okay Denise you got it! Go ahead mess up your life. Go right ahead with Joe Blow and be his wife. I don't care because you aren't listening to me anyway. Denise I love you and I know I can't stop you, so when Joe messes up, and believe me he will, you can come home. Oh…and baby you can find us at our new home in the suburbs."

"So I guess this means you're moving." "You got it! I am going to call Freddy in the morning and we will move at the end of this month. You will be graduating by then and you can make your own decision if you want to go with us or not." "Thanks for understanding mom." "The only thing I understand is that if that fool touches a hair on my baby heads or as much as hurts your feelings I will be in New York quicker than he can blink." "I know ma, I know." "You better know that I love you and I just want to see you have the best." "I know that too ma."

They both decided to go to sleep finally and Denise fell asleep in her mother's bed in her arms just like when she was a little girl. Denise loved her mom in spite of all the hard times they had with her. She knew her mom wanted better for them and Denise was tired of watching her struggle. She was so thankful that Freddy came along for her and she felt much better about New York and leaving her, Jeffrey and Jeanine alone.

Denise looked up to the ceiling and said, "God if you still here me or if you are still up there for me, please listen. I know I haven't been around for you and I am not a saint, but I do love you. I just wanted to say thank you for taking care of my mom and my brother and sister. Please watch over them while I am gone and watch over me as well. Amen…oh and God thanks for showing me your angel Todd."

(As Nina fell asleep she thought about Denise) She was still upset about Denise but she knew the more she rejected her decision the more she would pull away from her. After Nina slept on the thought of Denise leaving them she decided to let her go. She would have to find her own way in life and she wanted to be there for her. Calling Freddy to let him know they were coming to live with him was the first thing to do on Nina's list. When she woke up the next morning she reached over for the phone and dialed his number, "Hello Freddy, its Nina." "Hi baby, how did you sleep?"

"I slept well and I had a chance to think about us and I have to say yes to your offer." "You mean yes you will make a life with me! Yes you will be my woman and soon to be wife! Yes you and the kids will live with me happily ever after!" "Slow down, but yes…yes we will." "Oh Nina you have made me the happiest man alive. Let me take you and the kids out tonight for a celebration dinner and then I'll bring you back here so the kids can see their new house." "Okay that sounds good to me."

"Nina?" "Yes Freddy." "I do love you and I promise I will be the best man I can be for you. I will never hurt you or lie to you and I will respect you. I disrespected you before by sleeping with you just so you can get your rent paid and that was wrong. I know it may take me a lifetime to make up for that, but I am willing to try."

"I was wrong too. I don't blame you for anything. That is the past so let's leave it there." "That's fair but I still want to show you I love you for you and nothing else." "Well that's fine, you do that then." "When would you like to move in?" "I think at the end of the month. It will be the end of the school year and the kids can get settled in before they have to go to a new school. Denise will be going to New York." "Great! So she got accepted to NYU, that's wonderful." "No she didn't. Her little boyfriend did and she is following behind him thinking he is going to marry her so she is moving there with him."

"Denise you have to stop her. I will pay for her to go to college. This is crazy you can't let her ruin her life with some no good knuckle head." "I know…I know. I have already had this conversation with her and she won't listen to reasoning. I am going to let her go and find her own way. Freddy I am just afraid if I reject her she will leave me and never come back, I just couldn't take that. I am hoping she will get to New York and find out it isn't what she thought and then come home to get her life together."

"Baby I know that is what you think, and I am on your side but I don't know. Whatever you want to do, but I don't like him already." "Me either." "We are starting to sound more and more like a couple." (They both started to laugh, Hahaha) "Freddy we are a couple now." "Yeah that's right we are, aren't we? So you want me to go ruff him up for you baby?" "No, don't do that just hold me back from killing them both." (hahaha) "Nina I love you." "I love you back." "Do you mean it or are you just saying that to appease me?"

"I know I love your spirit and personality and you are the first man that has ever made me feel like a queen, the other night you made me feel like I was the most important person in the world. I love that about you and I don't want that to stop. I guess if loving you is wrong then I don't want to be right." (Haha) "Well if that's how you put it then we are just a couple in love." "Okay then, so what now?" "I will get a moving truck together for you and the kids at the end of this month and you don't worry about a thing. You tell me what you need and I'll get it. The only thing I want you to do is think about what you want to eat tonight." "I can handle that."

"Nina, don't worry about Denise she is a smart girl, she will find her way. When does she go to New York?" "I think right after the summer they are leaving." "I am going to make sure she has enough cash and has a place to stay down there, is that okay with you?"

"Freddy, I can't ask you to do that. You have done so much already." "Nina I plan on making you my wife once our relationship takes off, so that means that Denise is just like my step daughter. I can't see her out there in New York without any cash or a place to stay. I have to do it because she is your child and I love you, so I love her too." "Where did you come from? You must not be from this planet because no man I have ever known willingly takes on the responsibility of raising somebody's babies." "That's just it...I am not like any man you have ever known. I am going to show you that I can give you and the kids the world and all you have to do is be my woman, I love you that much." "Thanks for just being you Freddy." As they hung up the phone Nina was on cloud nine. She spent the rest of the day doing her hair and nails so she would look flawless for their evening dinner.

When Freddy came to pick them up that evening the kids decided they wanted seafood. Freddy spared no expense and the kids seemed to love him, even Denise. Nina was surprised at how well Denise and Freddy hit it off. Freddy knew a lot about the different colleges and he had been to New York before so they started talking about that. He was already acting like he was her father, telling her that boy better do right by her. After they finished dinner they headed to his house. Once they got there the kids were in awe at how big it was and so was Nina. This was the first time she had been in it and she was amazed at how clean it was for a man. He showed them the whole house and when the kids saw that each one of them had their own bedrooms and the rooms were huge, they fell out on the beds and begged Nina to stay.

Freddy showed Denise that she had her own room too and he told her that this was her home to come to whenever she wanted or needed to. Denise was really impressed with Mr. Freddy and his generosity. "Wow this is great Mr. Freddy. You have a really nice home." "No Denise, we have a really nice home. I want you kids to know that this is your home too, I mean it." As Nina looked around the house, she thought it was huge and a lot to maintain. Then she wondered who would have to clean it now that she wouldn't be working. "Well who do you think is going to clean this big house? I get it, that's why you want me to quit my job so I can cook and clean for you." "No Nina, I have a maid that comes in once a week. I do a lot of cooking myself so we can take turns cooking. If you don't want to quit your job you don't have too. I just think you can utilize your talents into something more rewarding." "I like the sound of that. You're right my talents can be used for other things. I never had a maid before...I like that idea."

(Denise was ecstatic for her mother and siblings) "I am so excited for you mom, you deserve all this after your hard work. Now Mr. Freddy I am counting on you to take care of my folks." "Baby girl you got my word as long as you take care of yourself too." "I will, no doubt." Jeffrey and Jeanine did not want to leave so they decided to spend the night and when they got up in the morning Mr. Freddy was already up making breakfast. Denise was the first one up, so she walked downstairs hoping to find some orange juice, instead she found Mr. Freddy cooking up a storm in the kitchen.

"What are you doing up so early it's the weekend?" "Good morning Denise, how did you like your room?" "It was great, thanks." "You like roller coasters?" "Yeah they're okay, I haven't been on one in awhile. Why?" "I thought it would be nice for us to go to the new amusement park they just built." "Today?" "Yes today, wouldn't that be fun?" "That is an hour drive or more." "I know, but who's keeping track of miles?" "Cool I'm game. I'll go wake Jeff and Jeanine up. I know they'll be excited." Denise ran upstairs to wake up the twins and when she told them they were going to the amusement park they jumped up screaming. "Hoorah! Yippe!" (Nina was awakened by the kids screams and shouts as she entered their bedroom) "Hey what is all the noise about in here?" (They all shouted) "Mr. Freddy is taking us to the amusement park today." "He is? Freddy! (Freddy came running upstairs as Nina called him) "Freddy!" "Yeah baby, what's up?" "You told the kids you were taking them to the park today?" "Yes and not just any park, the new amusement park up the coast. It has thirteen to die for roller coasters and all the kiddie rides you can think of."

"Hooray! Yippe! Yeah!" As the twins continued to run around screaming, Nina said, "Calm down Jeffrey and Jeanine we aren't there yet."(Freddy remembered he had made breakfast) "Let's go I made us a big breakfast downstairs and it's getting cold." As Freddy ran back downstairs, Denise grabbed her mother's hand and said, "Dag ma, you better keep him I like him." "Girl be quiet you too much." They all sat at the table and ate the biggest breakfast they ever had. Freddy had made steak, eggs, fruit, and toast and it was delicious. Then they all got dressed for the park and jumped in his truck and headed down the coast.

Once they got to the park the twins played and Freddy and Denise challenged each other on the roller coasters, Nina and the twins just laughed when they got off and they both looked sick. When they got back to the house it was late so Freddy took them home because they didn't have any more clothes at his house. "Nina I had a great time today with you and the kids. I want it to be that way all the time, I want us to be a family." "Me too." For the first time in years, Nina was happy. She enjoyed being with Freddy and she could tell the kids did too. She had gotten past the fact that he wasn't the muscle bound superstar husband that she wanted. What she had learned was that his heart was big enough to make her forget about whatever flaws she thought he had. In her eyes he had become a calm water in the midst of her troubles, a knight in shining armor, and a man that made her feel like she was cherished. Nina was sorry that she had wasted all these years being so silly about his looks and never giving him an opportunity to show her his heart. She had planned to be the very best wife she could be for Freddy, because she knew he was already everything she ever needed.

Chapter 7

Soul mates

It was a beautiful day and Todd was feeling truly blessed to have Lisa in his life. (Todd was looking out of his bedroom window as he thought about his new love) "We have become very close as friends and I know that she was sent to me by God. We have the same likes and dislikes and she seems to be very supportive of my future. This is the type of woman I have been asking God to bring into my life. Going to church and Bible study with her and being able to pray together has moved our relationship into such an awesome level. We have moved up even further in Christ and she has shown me what true love is all about. Because we are both walking with Christ a short kiss goodnight is as far as we have gotten and that is as far as we will go. I know that once she becomes my wife our love will be ordained by God and that will make it all the sweeter. I will ask her to marry me tonight. When I told my mother about my plans to marry her she was ecstatic and went with me to pick up the ring."

(Todd's thoughts were interrupted as his mother knocked on the door) "Todd, Lisa is on the phone." (He quickly picked the phone up) "Hi sweetie, how are you?" "I'm doing great and I am highly favored in the Lord. God bless you this morning, Todd." "God bless you too. I have a surprise for you." "You do! What is it?" "I can't tell you now." "So when?" "Tonight I will pick you up and take you to dinner and I will tell you then." "Oh really, I can't wait."

Todd was excited and so was his mother. He wanted to let Lisa know that she was the woman for him and that after they graduated they would be together as husband and wife. Even though he knew how they both felt about marriage and school, he wasn't sure if she would want to wait until after school or just get married now. Todd helped his mother in their yard all day. He cut the grass and she worked on her garden and they both planted new flowers. After a long hard day of yard work, he went to shower and change to get ready for his date. When Todd got to Lisa's house he was more nervous than he thought. As he knocked on the door he cleared his throat twice. Todd smiled as he saw Mr. McBride walking towards the door. He had already spoken to her parents last week about asking Lisa to marry him and they both gave him their blessing. "Good Evening son, come on in." "Good evening Mr. McBride." When Lisa heard the front door open she rushed downstairs to see Todd, because she couldn't wait for her surprise. "Bye Daddy, I'll see you later." "Okay baby you kids have fun. God bless you."

As soon as they got into the car Lisa turned toward Todd and said, "What is it?" "Dag sweetie, can we eat first?" "Okay and then you will tell me?" "Yes and then I will tell you." Todd drove to the oceanfront and parked the car and pulled out a picnic basket for them. Lisa watched as he laid the blanket down and took her hand and helped her sit down. He pulled out a white linen napkin and laid it across her lap and then pulled out a crab cake dinner from Jacob's Seafood House. Todd knew that was her favorite place to eat and she loved crab cakes. "Todd this is my favorite, so what's the special occasion?"

"The occasion is me loving you. When you approached me in the park I never knew we would become such good friends. You have shown me what being with a woman of God is like and I can't get enough of it. Praising our Father and loving him together has been such a blessing to me. I don't have a lot of close friends who love the Lord the way you do. Meeting a woman on the same accord as I am is rare. You are the woman I have been asking God to send me as a wife. You are the woman that I have been asking God to bless with me, to point me to scriptures in the Bible, to pray for me and with me. Will you grant me the honor and accept my hand in marriage?" (Todd waited for the helicopter to come across the sky with the banner that read: Lisa McBride will you marry me?)

Lisa looked up in the sky and saw the banner and started to cry. "Yes! Yes! Yes! I will marry you." He pulled out the ring and placed it on her finger and kissed her on the cheek. I know that we both have to think about school but you tell me what you want to do." "Well Todd, to be honest I do want to finish school, I have to finish school. Does that mean I can't be your wife?" "Of course not, I am already planning on going to college right after we graduate. I just want you to know I am yours forever. Why don't we just remain engaged and see where life takes us and God will tell us when the right time is to wed." "Todd you are so right. I know in my heart that you are the husband for me. There is no other man that I could ever want. I will wait for us for as long as it takes."

Todd was happy that Lisa agreed to make the commitment to be his future wife. He didn't want them to get married and loose their own identities in the process. If his wife wanted to go to Divinity School then he was going to support her 100%. Todd had already been accepted into Harvard and was planning on working on being a Pediatrician. He knew that Lisa was the wife he had been looking for and he didn't want to go off to school and leave their relationship unresolved. He felt so much better about leaving her knowing that she would be waiting when he got back home from school.

When Todd got home he felt so good about all his future plans. He couldn't sleep so he decided on a bowl of ice cream. As soon as Todd walked into the kitchen he noticed his mother was baking cookies as she said, "So how did it go?" "Hey ma…it went fine. What are you doing up cooking this late?" "I couldn't sleep so I decided to make some baked goodies to take to the shelter tomorrow. Well what did she say?" "She said yes." "Oh baby I'm so happy for you. I can't believe this…my baby boy is getting married. I am going to plan everything. I better call her mom so we can get together for lunch." "Mom we decided to remain engaged until after we finished college." "For four years?" "Well however long it takes." "Why wait so long? Son, she is a good catch. You know I am all for you finishing school but Todd you have enough in your account to buy that school. You can still be married and go to college. She can go to Divinity School anywhere and you can go to med school anywhere. Don't pass up a good woman.

Do you know how hard it is to find a woman after God's own heart, with a bright future like Lisa has? I have watched that child grow in the Lord from the time she was little and I can honestly say sister girl loves our Father like no other. She is pretty and intelligent, so what more could you ask for?" "I agree totally and that is why I have decided to wait. Mom I love her as much as you do and I want her to be able to experience things in life as a woman not just as my wife. I want her to be able to go to school like she planned before I came into the picture. I want her to know that just because a man loves her does not mean she has to drop her dreams for him. If our love is true it will stand the test of time. Only God knows what he has for me is for me. No man shall take that away or can take it away. If she is still there when we both are ready to start our life together then bless the Lord. But if she is not, then bless the Lord for allowing such a wonderful person into my life for just a moment.

Lisa does not know that we are wealthy, nor do I want her to know until she is my wife. My wealth was given to me because of my father's death and that is not how I wanted to get rich. I will use that money to bless other people and I know that my father would still want me to sacrifice to make my own riches." "We raised you well baby. Your daddy was a good man and I know that he would be so proud of you right now. I guess I let my excitement get the best of me. I lost sight of the true meaning of love. You're right honey, if Lisa is the one for you she will be here for you when you get back." "Thank you ma."

The weekend was over and it was back to hitting the books at school. They only had one day left to be seniors and then the real challenged started with college. All the seniors at school were walking on cloud nine because graduation day was coming up. Todd still considered Denise as a friend and he knew that today was her birthday so he decided to stick a birthday card in her locker. As he walked through the crowded hallway he spotted her in the corner by her locker hugged up with that creep Joe. Denise didn't look like she was happy. In fact she was pushing Joe away as Todd heard her yell, "Joe stop it!" Joe was being very persistent, "Come on Denise give me another kiss." "People are starting to stare, Joe." "So what…let em look. You are my girl and I don't care who knows. That's right everybody, this is my baby." As Joe kissed Denise all over her face Todd started to feel sorry for her. He knew Joe was a creep but Denise couldn't see it. Now she was mixed up with him and Todd didn't see her leaving the situation anytime soon. Joe kissed her one last time before he turned to walk away, "Look here baby I got to get to class so I'll see you after school."

As Joe turned the corner he didn't see Todd so Todd just turned his head. Todd saw Claire watching Joe from the corner of her eye and once he got around the corner she walked past Joe and patted him on the butt. He just turned around and smiled at her. Todd thought to his self Joe is such a dog and he should tell Denise, but he knew she wouldn't listen to him. Todd thought his birthday card might cheer her up as he walked towards her trying to put on a big smile as if he hadn't just witnessed that ugly display of affection from Joe.

"Happy Birthday Denise!" "Todd you startled me, thank you. I can't believe you remembered." "Well that's what friends are for, right?" "Right you are...thanks for the card that was very sweet of you." "No biggie, that's what I am a sweet guy. So have you decided what you are going to do after graduation?" "Actually Joe and I are getting married and moving to New York. I know you don't like him but we love each other." "You are doing what! Girl, are you crazy? Joe is the biggest dog in this town. Why are you the only one who can't see that?" "He used to be...so I heard, but he is not like that anymore. Joe has changed and he is committed to me." "Denise I hate to be the one to break the news to you, but Joe just let Claire pat him on the butt going down the hall, so you call that committed?" "Joe did what with Claire? First I am going to cut her up in pieces and then I'm going to spit her out. How dare her touch my man on his butt."

Todd didn't mean for that to slip out but he wanted to expose Joe for the rascal that he was. He watched Denise walk down the hallway looking for Claire and he just shook his head as he ran after her. "Denise! Denise!

Violence begets violence. You don't need to confront Claire, you need to confront Joe." "Todd, right now I am not trying to hear your Jesus peace offerings." "Denise calm down, all I'm saying is that Joe is the one that put you and Claire in the middle of this. You need to stop and think about that. If this man is planning on being your husband then he needs to be held accountable for his actions." Denise was listening to Todd, but she thought he was too hard on Joe. "Now I see what's going on. You still want me and you are making up this story about Joe so we will break up. You think this will make me stay here so I can be with you." "No I'm sorry you're wrong about that.

Look, I was just being honest and trying to help out a friend." "You had this all planned out didn't you?" "Denise, stop being a fool and open your eyes the guy is bad news. Take my advice I don't need to lie on him to make him look bad, he does that on his own." "This is my future husband you are talking about. Take that back! I know you are doing this to break us up because you want me to be with you." "Denise I am engaged to another woman. I plan to marry her after we graduate college. I use to have feelings for you outside of a friendship, but when I found out you were back with Joe all that changed. I respect your relationship with Joe and I respect you as a woman and a friend. I just want what's best for you. I don't want to see you get hurt."

"You're engaged! You're engaged to who?" "Her name is Lisa McBride." "So where did you meet this Ms. Lisa McBride?" "She attends my church and I have known her for quite a few years. We just recently developed an interest in each other." "Oh…I see you just recently developed this interest and you just recently got engaged?" "Well yes, if you want to put it like that, what about you?" "What about me?" "You are also engaged." "You're right, I am but I never figured that you would be too." "Now what is that suppose to mean. You think because I love the Lord I can't love a woman?"

"No, that is not what I mean. I just didn't know that you had any other love interest." "Oh…I get it you thought because you hurt my feelings by being with Joe that I was going to crawl up under a rock and wait for Denise to decide that Joe was a loser and come back to me." "No, not that either…I don't know what I thought.

I suppose now that you have your godly woman you won't be around as a friend for me?" "See Denise that is where you are confused. My God comes first and my wife comes second but I will always have time for a friend. My wife can also be your friend." "Not interested" "Look, I will have no secrets from her about anything or anyone in my life. I can support you and advise you the best way I know how. What I do know is that Joe is no good and marrying him is a bad move. Now you see that it has nothing to do with me wanting to be with you at all. I just want you to know that you deserve better. God will shine his light on you and in time he will reveal things to you. You have to put yourself in a position to receive them. God Bless you Denise."

When Todd walked down the hallway he prayed to God he would show Denise the light before she went to New York with that fool. Todd knew that no one else could show her but God. She had to learn on her own and he had a feeling she was going to learn the hard way. Todd had thought in the beginning that Denise was his soul mate. He could see that she had

God's love in her. He thought all he needed to do was help her bring it out. Now he thought maybe he was wrong.

Chapter 8

Temptations

Denise was so angry with Todd for accusing Joe of being a dog that she wanted to smack him, but instead she decided to prove him wrong. She planned on making sure her and Joe had the perfect relationship and she was determined to get her nursing degree. Denise went to the library and pulled up all the schools in New York that had anything to do with nursing. She found one she really liked and called the registration office to find out about admission. The tuition was way over her head and she felt like the situation was hopeless. The counselor told her she could apply for financial assistance so she decided to do that. Denise couldn't wait to tell her mom about it when she got home.

They were living with Mr. Freddy now and Freddy and her mom were getting very close. Denise thought it was nice to see her mom happy. As she walked in the door she sang out loud, "I'm home and I have good news." "Hey Denise what's up?" "Hey Mr. Freddy, where is ma?" "She went to the store, she will be back soon…so what is this good news?" "I'll wait for momma." (Denise was interrupted by her mother walking in the door with her arms full of shopping bags) "Hey baby, help me with these bags." "What did you buy?" "Girl, Saks had a sale so I got you some going away clothes and I got myself some staying at home clothes, and I got the twins some school clothes. Oh, and baby I got you some nice dress shirts."

Freddy quickly ran over to kiss Nina as he said, "Thanks baby, I'll get the bags for you." "I have some good news mom." "Well I like good news, so what's up? Wait! Don't tell me. You came to your senses and you're not moving to New York with Joe Blow." "No ma and his name is Joe Turner."

"Yeah whatever, if he mess with my baby his last name better be Blow because he gonna need somebody to blow his hind parts off the face of this earth. Don't play with my babies, I'll cut somebody." "Ma! Would you cut it out for a moment. You promised you would respect my decision." "Okay, you right. I'm sorry now give me your news."

"I found a good nursing school in New York and I filled out the financial aid papers and I'm sure I can get it. I can go there at night and work during the day. I also filled out a few applications online and sent my resume off. I think I have a good chance at getting a job down there in no time." Freddy looked at Nina and then he looked at Denise, "Financial Aid? Baby how much does this school cost?" "Mr. Freddy I am not asking for your money, I can handle it." "I said how much baby girl?" "Its ten thousand dollars, but it's just a crash course."

"Ten thousand dollars! With the interest on a student loan you will have to pay back twenty thousand when you done, I'll give you the money." "I can't ask you to do that." "Okay then fine…but me and your mama went out and got you a graduation gift. The gift comes with the money, but you have to take both or no deal." "What graduation gift?" "It's out back, go see."

Freddy and Nina were both grinning like kids at Christmas time. Denise looked at her mother and noticed she was almost in tears. Then she looked at Mr. Freddy and walked towards the garage out back. There it was…a bright red Volkswagon Jetta. "Is this for me?" "Yes baby can you believe it, your very own car!"

Nina was more excited than Denise was as she said, "I told Freddy that it was too much but he insisted that every girl should get a car on their eighteenth birthday." Denise hugged Mr. Freddy while she wiped tears from her eyes. "Thank You. I don't know what to say." "Well you said it baby girl, now first thing Monday morning we will take you to get your driver's license so you can drive the thing." "Yes sir!"

Denise hugged them both again as tight as she could and ran upstairs to call Joe to tell him the good news. (Denise waited as the phone rang twice) "Hello." "Joe…guess what!" "What?" "I got a new car." "Stop playin, are you for real?" "Yes, Mr. Freddy bought it for me. It's a Volkswagon Jetta. It's red and it is brand new."

"Come pick me up and let's go for a ride." "I have to get my license first." "I knew your mom's was strict, she don't play that." "Plus I got into this nursing school in New York." "You did?" "Yes and it's close to NYU, but where will we live?" "I got an apartment not far from the campus. It's a one bedroom and you know New York is expensive, so it's small." "If it's with you I don't care what size it is. Joe I am so excited about us making this move together." "Me too, baby."

"I have been meaning to ask you something." "What is it baby?" "Did Claire pat you on your butt?" "What do you mean, recently or a long time ago?" "What I mean is…did she ever pat you on the butt?" "Denise baby…Claire is history. Why you keep bringing up the past? It's me and you baby, Claire means nothing to me." "Joe I need to know that you are going to be committed to me and me only when we go to New York."

"Denise haven't I been with you for most of our senior year? Didn't I ask you to marry me and move to New York with me? Why are you trippin? I love you not Claire. Would you rather I ask her to come with me?" "No Joe, that is not what I am saying." "Then what are you saying, because right now you are acting like you don't want to be with me?" "Joe you know I want to be with you, why are you doing this?"

"All I'm saying is, don't be questioning me like I am some child. You're going to be my wife, not my mother." "I'm sorry I didn't mean to sound like your mother. It's just that sometimes I feel like you are calling all the shots and I am just being added into the mix after the fact. I just want to be included in our lifelong decisions." "I do include you. Here I am rearranging my whole life for you to be in it and this is the thanks I get." "I didn't ask to come to New York you asked me. If you feel like I am such a burden then I can stay here in Philly and make my own life. You haven't even given me a proper proposal yet, what happened to my ring? What happened to you getting down on one knee for me? Then I have to hear all these accusations about you and Claire. I have been there for you and stood up for you no matter what other people said about you. I had to defend you to my mother and my friends. I am the one rearranging my life, not you." (Denise began to cry) "I am such a fool, baby. You're right I have been so selfish in this relationship. I love you more than anything. I don't mean to take you for granite.

Denise, please don't tell me that you're not going with me. I can't make it if you don't go. You have supported me and you have believed in me when I didn't believe in myself. Can I come see you for a minute? I have something special for you. I was going to wait until we got to New

York but I want you to have it now. Please stop crying baby. I promise I will make everything up to you. When we get to New York you will see. You will see how much I love you." "So what is this special thing you have for me?" "I'm on my way."

Denise could sense that there were some things that Joe needed to work on with his temper, but she thought she was willing to do whatever it took to make their relationship work. If Joe was going to be her husband she had to stand by his side. As she freshened up waiting for Joe to arrive she was curious to know what Joe had for her. She was also ready to let him know that Denise Combs was not to be played with. She had been submissive to him all this time, but she knew she had to let him know she was a strong willed woman. She had a piece of her mind to give him in person when he got there.

As Denise heard the doorbell ring she rushed downstairs to get it before her mother. (Ding Dong) "I got it!" "Who is at the door, Denise?" "It's Joe, ma." (Denise's mother came rushing out of the family room to the front door) "Oh I want to meet this fellow. Well hello Joe...so what you plan on doing with my daughter in New York?"

"Good afternoon Ms. Combs, nice to see you. "Cut the crap...like I said what do you plan on doing with my daughter in New York?" "Momma, please stop it!" Joe was getting a little nervous so he decided to turn on his irresistible charm.

"Denise I think your mama has a good point. She doesn't know me so she has every right to question me. Ms. Combs I plan on making your daughter the happiest woman in New York. I plan on loving her and respecting her. I plan on making her my wife and someday the mother of my children. I only want to love her, that's all." Denise was smiling from ear to ear and she was so proud that Joe put on some nice clothes and his best behavior in front of her mother. As Denise hugged Joe she noticed her mother had a frown on her face as she said, "She may fall for those lines but I'm from the old school. I know one thing, if I find out that she so much as breaks a nail out there because of you…boy I will beat you down." "Momma…please stop that. Joe is going to be my husband so can you show a little respect?" Freddy walked up behind Nina and placed his hands on her shoulders as he eye balled Joe. "The boy better know about respect. My name's Freddy and you see this here little girl?" "Yes sir!" "Don't even think about mistreating her. You better come correct son or don't come back around here no more." "Mr. Freddy…Momma, both of you just stop it! Enough is enough I am eighteen now so just cut it out.

Freddy grabbed Nina's hand and motioned her to walk over to the family room. Denise watched them both walk back into the other room and Mr. Freddy walked backwards with his eyes on Joe. Denise was so embarrassed but she knew they both loved her. After they were out of sight Denise turned towards Joe and said, "Now that we have gotten through that ordeal, what did you want to show me?" Joe looked like he was scared to death and speechless. He pulled a tiny red box out of his back pocket and laid it in Denise's hand as she felt him trembling.

Denise started to kiss him so he would feel at ease and then Joe relaxed and held her close to him. "Denise Combs, will you marry me?" "Yes silly, I already told you yes." Joe got down on one knee and proposed to her again and Denise just got down on the floor and melted into his arms.

The summer had gone by so fast and Denise couldn't believe that she was finally a high school graduate. She was packing her stuff to move to New York with Joe when her mother came in. "The twins are sure gonna miss you. Not to mention the fact that this place won't be the same without you. Denise, are you positive this is what you want?" "Yes mama it is. This is not goodbye...it's just see you later. I will probably be up here so much visiting you guys that you will be sick of me. You know I need my twin fix. I love those two little munchkins to death." "Freddy and I have decided to take you down and get you settled in." "That is not necessary mother. I love you both but let me do this by myself, please."

(They were interrupted by the doorbell ringing) That must be Joe. I better hurry up before Mr. Freddy puts him in a choke hold." Nina grabbed Denise tight and the twins rushed in and hugged her and slobbered kisses all over her face. After they all finally let Denise up she was soaking wet from kisses and could hardly breathe. "I will be back for Thanksgiving that is not very far away. Jeffrey and Jeanine why don't we make an X on the calendar each week, and that way you will know when it is getting close to the time for me to come home."

"Okay Nisey we will and I will make a big red X for you because that is the same color as your car." "That's right Jeanine!" "My X will be blue because blue is for boys." "Yes Jeff, blue is a boys color but I like it too."

They both grabbed her neck and held her tight and her mother wrapped her arms around all of them and Denise and Nina started to cry so hard that they couldn't stop. As Denise tried to let go of them she realized she was holding them just as tight as they were holding her. "I have to go now...let me go munchkins…Nisey has to go bye bye." Nina wiped her tears and said, "Come on guys let Nisey go, don't worry we will see her soon.

"Mommy, why she got to go? (Jeff looked at his mother with an innocent face) We just got a new house. Don't you like our new house Nisey? Don't you like Mr. Freddy? We promise we will be good, please don't leave us?" Denise was so broken up over the twins not wanting her to go that she couldn't speak. She never thought it would hurt this much to leave them. "No Jeff everything is fine. I like our new house and I like Mr. Freddy, but it's time for Nisey to be a grown up now. I have to go and make a life for myself. That doesn't change the way I feel about you and Jeanine. I love you both more than anything and I will always be your big sis. I will always be here for you. I promise I will be back and I will call you every night." "Will you read the Happy Time Bear story to us over the phone?" "Yes Jeanine if you want me to, I will." "Okay if you promise to keep your promise you can go." "I promise and I cross my heart." "I love you sis." "I love you both with all my heart."

Once Denise got downstairs she could tell Mr. Freddy had drilled Joe again. She handed her bags to Joe and he hurried to put them in the car. She wanted to say one last goodbye to Mr. Freddy and momma so she let Joe go outside to load the car up. Denise could tell Mr. Freddy didn't want her to go as he said, "Well baby girl this is your big step.

I want you to know I will take the best of care of your momma and your sister and brother. I am always here for you if you need help or fall short. You understand me?" "Yes Mr. Freddy and thank you for everything." "Well it aien't nothing. Don't you let no man dictate your life for you, you hear me?" "Yes sir!" "You get to New York and you show em what Denise

Combs is made of. You get out there and be the best nurse you can be. I don't want you out there struggling because you aien't got to. You can always come home." "I know Mr. Freddy." "Here take this." Mr. Freddy slipped an envelope in her hand and she looked in it and there was so much cash that her eyes almost popped out of her head. She had never seen so much money in her life.

"I know it aien't much but three thousand should tie you over for a little while. Don't be frivolous with your money and definitely don't give it to that boy, that's for you. If he wants to be a man then let him get out there and show me he can survive like a man." "Three thousand dollars! This is a lot of money!" "Baby girl once you start paying rent and paying bills you gonna see that aien't really no money at all. If you need more then call us. For now get yourself on your feet. Me and your momma called that nursing school to make sure it was legit." "You did?" "You know your momma got to check everything out. We went ahead and paid it off for you." "You did! You guys are too much. I can't believe you did that for me." "We didn't want you in some strange city worrying about making ends meet and trying to get money for tuition." "Thanks!" Denise hugged Mr. Freddy tight and waved goodbye to her family and her new house.

As Denise got in the car she looked out the window wondering if she was making the right decision. She could tell Joe was a little frustrated. "Finally, I thought we would never get out of there." "You know my family, they are concerned." "Oh yeah…well I got you to myself now." Joe leaned over and playfully kissed Denise and rubbed her face gently. Even though she had her doubts she felt good and she knew they were meant to be together she was just a little nervous. The ride to New York was long and tiring, when they got to the apartment Denise was exhausted. Joe drove up to a building that looked like it was abandoned. He got out the car and told her to follow him. As they approached the apartment door, he waved his hand in front of it as he said, "Here we are." "This is it?" "I know it doesn't look like much now, but we can fix it up." "Joe this looks like a roach motel." "Don't be so skeptical, you are lacking vision. Look at the big picture. You can put some nice covers on the couch with some throw pillows, or we could paint it. What about some curtains?"

"Joe we hardly have a window, why do we need curtains?" "See there you go again looking at the negative side of everything. I am trying to do my best. I told you, New York was expensive, this is all I could afford." "I'm sorry, maybe once we rearrange some things we can go to the store and purchase some stuff that will make the place homey." "We don't have money for that. We have to make due with the stuff we have." "I do have a little money. Plus I can't sleep in this place until we fix it up and get some bombs for these roaches."

"Cool! You got the cash so let's go." They got to the store and purchased new sheets and pillow cases. Denise got some other items to dress the place up and bought a can of paint. She was excited about their new place and she wanted it to look special. Joe had an interview for a part time job the next day so she decided to work on the apartment all day until she got it the way she wanted it. Denise worked all day painting, washing walls, and rearranging furniture. She was almost done when she heard Joe walk in the door. "Baby this looks like a new place. You are incredible! How did you do all this by yourself?" "I had help from motivation, ambition, and down right determined." "I love it, it looks great." Joe grabbed Denise in his arms and started to kiss her gently and then he became more intense. As Denise kissed him back harder he pulled her overalls off her shoulders. She loved kissing him but she was still sticking to her guns about waiting until they were married to go any further.

Her overalls fell down by her ankles and he started to touch her breast. "Joe I think we should stop." "I am just getting started, baby. Let's go to the bedroom, I can't wait to see what you did in there." Joe moved Denise towards the bedroom while he kissed her and fondled her all over her body. It felt good but she knew she had gone too far this time. "Joe! I said stop it!" "What is your problem, just relax?" "You know how I feel about this." "I know how you felt, but its different now. We are living together so what difference does it make now. Mommy isn't going to creep around the corner, she's in Philly. So come on and stop teasing me." "I am not teasing you, I love you but I can't." (Joe pushed Denise away from him) "Why Denise, why can't you make love to me? I have waited for this and now that we are living together you still can't do this. I want to know why right now!"

"My virginity is all I have, it is all that I own. It is all that belongs to Denise Combs and I can't give it up to anybody." "Oh, so I'm just anybody now? I thought I was your fiancé?" "You are, but you aren't my husband."

"What is this...some Christian belief that fool Todd was feeding you?" "This has nothing to do with Todd or being a Christian, this is just how I feel." "Well you know if you are such a virgin you shouldn't be shackin up with a guy that aien't your husband." "So you want me to leave now?" "Did I say that?" "Joe this is not about any Christian belief. I moved here with you because I thought we would be getting married soon. By the way when is our wedding?" "Don't play games with me girl. I told you once we get on our feet we would have a wedding." "Why can't we just go to the Justice of the Peace?" "I don't want that, I want our day to be special. We will have our day soon I promise."

"At first you said we could go to the Justice of the Peace, now you have changed your story. I am sick of your promises I want to know now." Joe could tell Denise wasn't backing down this time. He wanted to calm her down before she decided to go back home. "Come here sweetie." Denise walked over to Joe and he reached out for her and placed her on his lap. "I'm trying to make this right for us. I got the job today so things are starting to look up." "You did! That is wonderful, I am so proud of you." "Can you let me be a man here and just make our way in this big city first? Then we will get married. I want you to have the white dress, bridesmaids and all the flowers you can stand."

"Baby that sounds nice, but all I want is you. I love you and I need you to respect how I feel." "Baby I do respect you." Joe started to kiss Denise again longer and deeper and she was starting to feel mesmerized. "I respect us baby and I need to know that you really love me." "You know I love you." "No I don't."

"But I always tell you I love you." "Actions speak louder than words, you need to show me. Prove your love to me and break this one rule. If you do it for me I will know that you are really my woman for life." "You can't ask me to do this, this isn't fair Joe. Once we are married I will show you." Joe continued to kiss her as he moved his hands down her thighs once he touched her inner thigh Denise grabbed his hand and pulled him away. Joe was outraged he just knew that once he got Denise away from her mother she would give up her virginity to him. "Don't you ever do that!" (Joe grabbed Denise's wrist) Denise couldn't believe that Joe had her wrist twisted and was yelling at her. "Don't you ever yank my hand away from you. I brought you all the way out here and you mean to tell me that you still not going to give me none."

Denise pulled away from Joe and ran towards the door. He grabbed her by her hair as she was turning the lock and knocked her down. She kicked and screamed hoping a neighbor would hear her, but no one came to her rescue. Joe pulled Denise underneath him and ripped her shirt. "Why you make me take it like this? This is not how it is suppose to be Denise. Why do I have to make my woman have sex with me?"

As Joe tried to position her body underneath him she continued to toss and turn. Denise kicked Joe so hard he was seeing stars. She jumped up and made it to the door and grabbed her purse on the way out. She looked back and watched him bending over holding his stomach. When Denise got outside there were taxi's everywhere so she jumped in one of them. "Take me to the nearest hotel, please." The driver dropped her off five blocks down the street and she checked into the hotel.

Once she got in the room she fell out on the bed crying. "That bastard! My mother was right. Todd was right. Everybody was right, but me. I should have known he was no good." Denise wanted to call her mother but she couldn't tell her this, it would break her heart. Plus she would probably be up here in the morning with a hit out on Joe. She figured she just needed to cool off and rest so she could think things through. The next morning when Denise got up she had the worst headache. She went to take a shower hoping that would calm her down.

After her shower she started to feel a little better and then she heard someone knocking on her door. (Knock, Knock) "Who could this be? No one knows I'm here." "Room service." "But I didn't ask for room service." "Well someone must like you because they ordered a full course breakfast that has been paid in full for you." "What was their name?" "I didn't get names just cash. Now do you want this food or not? I have other deliveries to make?" "Just leave it outside." "As you wish." Denise waited to hear the elevators to make sure he was gone. She looked outside and the hallway was empty. She was starving so she pulled the tray in the room as quickly as she could. Denise was struggling with the big tray of food, so she propped the door open. As soon as she got the tray inside and began to shut the door, Joe pushed his way inside. "Please here me out." "How did you find me? I should have known it was you who sent me breakfast. Look there is nothing for you to say. I can't believe you almost tried to rape me last night, it's over between us. I can't live with you after what you did to me." "I can't blame you, but please here me out first."

"You have two minutes and then I am throwing you out." "Denise we have been together for almost a year now and I have watched you and adored everything about you. I have been with a woman before and I know what it's like to be intimate with someone you care about. The thing is I have never loved anyone like you. I desire you more and more every time I see you. I have held back my desire because I knew you were a virgin. I guess I let my feelings for you get out of hand. I just wanted to be able to touch you and hold you without any restrictions. When I came home and saw that you had made our home so lovely it made me love you even more. You are the perfect wife for me. You can't understand what it's like for a man to have the woman he loves right next to him and not be able to enjoy her. I can barely kiss you because I know I will want more. Denise I desire you so much it hurts. It hurts me because you don't feel the same way."

"That's not true." "Denise I feel like we were just starting to make a life out here. Please don't give that up so quickly. Please don't give up on me so quickly. I know I don't deserve you and what I did was unforgivable. I am ashamed of myself right now. I have been looking for you all night. I have gone to every hotel around here, can we try again?" "Joe I do love you but how do I know this won't happen again?" "I won't be as stupid as I was again. Let's just get married next month. We will go to the Justice of the Peace like you said and we can have a nice ceremony down the line." "Really!" "That is if you still want me. I will never hurt you again and I have held out this long for you so I can wait another month. I just want to get a month's worth of paychecks and get settled in at school first. Is that okay with you, baby?"

"Yes that is fine, I should have been more understanding. I know it must be hard for you being a man and all. It is hard for me too. I do want you and I do love you, but I want our love to be explored after we are married." "Okay Mrs. Turner you got it. I promise I will never do that to you again." Joe pulled out a gold charm bracelet and put it around her wrist. "I hurt your wrist so I wanted to incase it in gold. I will never hurt you again anywhere. I am so sorry I acted like such a fool last night, please forgive me." Denise grabbed Joe and hugged him close and they both cried in each others arms. She knew their relationship was going to take a lot of work. But she was willing to take the time to make things better. Denise thought once they were married things would be so different. Their love would be concealed, Joe's anger would subside, and life would be wonderful.

She just had to give Joe his space so that he could prove his man hood and make his way in life. After he began working and she started school things would start to get back on track. The important thing was that they loved each other. Denise forgave Joe for what he did, because she thought everyone makes mistakes. She figured she should have known that it would be hard for them to live together without being intimate. That was a lot to ask of any man. Denise thought the fact that he lasted this long proved he really loved her. Denise saw how her mother used her body to get what she wanted and she wasn't going that route. The only man she ever wanted touching her in that way was her husband and that was final. Denise had conditioned her mind to believe that was her only weapon in life and she wanted to use it wisely. Denise had seen other girls reputations ruined and she was determined it would never happen to her. So if she had to be known as a good girl, then so be it.

Chapter 9

Joy comes in the Morning

As Nina looked out of the window she started to think about Denise. She thought it seemed so quiet around here without her. Nina called her every night and Denise assured her things were going just fine. But every time Nina and Freddy tried to plan a trip to come and see her, she made up excuses. Nina didn't trust that boy anyway. Next weekend she planned on going up there whether Denise liked it or not. (Freddy walked up behind Nina and grabbed her around the waist) "Baby why you standing here staring out the window, what's wrong?" "Oh nothing…just missing Denise." "You want to go see her today?" "No, they probably have classes today and work this evening. I'm fine…really. I knew sooner or later she had to leave me, but I guess I never thought it would be like this."

"Well if you don't want to go and see her then what can I do to lift your spirits up?" "Nothing, I told you I'm fine." "Will you be my wife?" "You ask me that every day." "Yes and everyday you give me a playful answer and beat around the bush. I know how a woman acts when she is in love with you and I can tell you have fallen in love with me." "You're right Freddy, I have. I tell you how much I love you everyday. You have been wonderful to me and the kids and I do love you, I love you very much. I have been so caught up with trying to prevent this marriage from happening between Denise and Joe that I can't sleep, eat or think straight. I have been distant from you since she left. I am just worried about her and I know there is nothing I can do. I am putting our relationship on hold for another relationship that I can't control. I am so sorry baby, please forgive me."

"I know and that is why I gave you your space. I am right here with you baby. I am concerned about Denise too. But we can't stop living because she has started to grow up. Our love has just begun and it gets even better. Nina, I want to show you and the kids the world. I want to be a father to them and a husband to you. You can have it all baby, but you got to let go of some stuff and let me into your heart."

Nina loved this man more than she thought she could. He had been a shelter in a raging storm for her and she was so thankful to him. Nina didn't know why she hadn't said yes to all his proposals up until now. She knew at this very moment that no man could love her like he did. She thought she would be a fool not to be his wife. "Yes sweetheart I will marry you." "Nina do you mean it baby?" "With all my heart I mean it." Freddy carried Nina upstairs and they made love all day and talked about their wedding plans in the bed in each other's arms. Nina decided that she wanted a small gathering at the house, nothing fancy. Freddy said she could have whatever she wanted.

Freddy was so excited and he wanted to tell the kids the good news so he said, "The kids will be getting out of school soon, why don't we go pick them up?" "No...I want to stay right here in your arms. The bus will bring them home." "I can't wait to tell them the good news and then we can go out for dinner. Plus I want to stop by Tiffany's so you can pick out your ring." "Oh...well if you put it that way then let's go." "You a trip, you know that?" "I was just kidding." "Yeah right!" "No seriously I was. I know at first the attraction may have had something to do with the money, but I feel different now. I have grown to love you more than you could ever understand.

I don't want you to get me a big fancy ring just to prove your love to me. You have already done that in more ways than one. I see how you love me, and how you have accepted and loved my children just like your own, I can't replace that. I would never try and replace that. I think two matching gold bands would be nice. Besides I've spent enough of your money already." Freddy pulled Nina back down in the bed and held her close. "You are a woman after my own heart. But my woman will be wearing a rock on her finger if it's the last thing I do." Freddy kissed Nina on her forehead then he kissed her on her cheek. He moved his lips around her face like it was a map. As they made love again Nina started to cry tears of joy and he just held her tighter and tighter as he playfully licked her tears from down her face.

Reluctantly they got out of bed when they heard the twins coming in from school and rushed to get dressed. When they told them their good news they were so excited. They were even more excited when they found out they were going out to dinner. When they got home from dinner Nina's first priority was to call Denise. "Hello Joe is Denise home?" "No Ms. Combs she had class. She should be home around ten tonight." "Well what is going on with you guys? We need to come out there to see you soon." "Yes maam you do, we are both working now. Denise works at the doctor's office from nine to five and then she goes to class at night from six to ten. She said she likes her job even though she is just doing filing. She is trying to learn the ropes by watching the other nurses." "That's wonderful, she didn't tell me." "I think she wanted to get settled in first." "Well how are her classes going?"

"She loves it! It's a lot of hard work and she is usually up studying pretty late, but she said it's worth it." "Well how are you two doing?" "We are doing fine." "Now that I have the update on my baby, what is going on with you?" "Oh me…I'm going to school full time and then I wait tables at night at the Doonsberry." "The Doonsberry, what is that?" "It's a local bar, but the tips are really good." "A bar…MMHHH. Well anyway me and Freddy want to come out and see you guys this weekend, do you have plans?"

"Actually I was coming up there this weekend to see my mom." "Good, then why don't you all stop by here I would love to meet your mom anyway." "Well Denise is staying here. She said she had to work this weekend." "Well when can she have any fun? That girl is going to work herself to death." "She only works one weekend out of a month, so that is why I planned to come up there this weekend." "Well what about the following weekend?" "Sure…that would be great I know Denise will be excited. I'll tell her to call you when she gets in tonight." "Yes you do that, will you?" "Yes." "Okay, talk to yall later."

Joe put the phone on the receiver and said, "Whew! That was a close one. I'm glad I got out of that. I wasn't trying to see Denise's folks this weekend. I am going up to Philly to see my family and hopefully get some from Claire." Joe had called Claire last week to let her know he would be in town and she was all for it. Then Joe thought about Denise, he loved Denise but this good guy profile was not him. Joe was glad he worked late at night because he didn't want Denise to know that the bar he worked at had strippers on Friday nights. She would have freaked out and overreacted.

As Joe heard Denise coming through the front door he walked over to greet her. "Hey honey how was class?" "Long and tiring…I am pooped and I have an exam tomorrow." "Your mom called." "She did! What did she say?" "She said they wanted to come down this weekend, but I told her you had to work." "I would love to see them too, but this weekend is hectic for me. You won't be here anyway, you will be up there." "I know that's what I told her." "Why don't you wait for me to get off Saturday and we can ride up together, I am off on Sunday."

"I thought you said you were going to have to study all day Sunday?" "Yes I do, but I could study while you drive." "Denise I had plans with some buddies on Saturday and me and my mom were going to do something Saturday evening together. I want to get home early on Sunday to get ready for school Monday morning." (Denise was very disappointed, because she missed her mom) "I understand, I guess another time."

"Baby I'm sorry. This is just not a good weekend for this. Your mom said they will come down the following weekend and we can all plan to do something nice together." Denise was almost in tears, so she turned around and leaned on the kitchen counter to hide her disappointment from Joe. Then Joe grabbed her from behind and hugged her waist while he kissed her on the neck. Denise grabbed Joe's arms and thought about how good he felt. Whenever he touched her, her heart began to melt. "Okay that's fine Joe." "Thank you sweetie."

Denise decided she would be okay after she talked to her mom, so she went to the living room and picked up the phone to call her. It was late but she just needed to hear her voice. The phone rang several times before anyone picked it up. (Nina struggled to get up as she reached for the phone) "Who could this be at this time of night? Hello, who is this?" "It's me momma." "Baby, hi! How you doing? I miss you so much and the twins miss you and Freddy misses you." "Me too momma…I miss you guys a lot. But things are going well. School is tough but I am learning so much. You won't believe this but I have a job! I am working as a filing clerk in one of the local clinics. The nurses are really cool and they know I am trying to get my nursing degree so they always let me watch them work. Everyone has been so nice." "Good baby, I'm happy for you. It sounds like things are coming together out there for you."

"Joe told me you guys wanted to come this weekend, but things are just too hectic right now. The following weekend we will both be off and we can show you around New York." "That sounds great we'll be there. I was calling to let you know that Freddy has asked me to marry him." "Well what else is new? The man has asked you everyday since you have been with him." "I haven't been that bad, but this time I said yes. Denise I really do love him and he is such a good man. So I need your blessing. The twins already told me it was okay, so what do you say?"

"I say heck yeah! Are you crazy? The man has won my vote by a land slide and if you don't marry him you would be nuts." "Thank you baby." "When will this gala affair take place? I'm sure he has rented some extravagant hall somewhere."

"No nothing like that I just want a small family gathering with us here at the house. The minister will come and we can say our vows and then we will have dinner. I don't want nothing fancy, I'm too old for all that." "You are not too old. You have been a perfect size 10 since we were kids and you look better than most of the twenty year olds I know.

Mom you look good and you deserve to walk down the aisle on the white carpet just as much as any young woman does." "Well thank you sweet pea I do try my best. But I prefer something intimate and small. We don't have much family here, except for a few friends. I am not about to cater to the rest of my fake family that has to come out of town just to see how big my ring is. Especially since they barely call to see how we are doing. Plus Freddy's parents are deceased and he is an only child. I just prefer something intimate and small."

"Whatever you say." "Plus I need to start planning your wedding right? Or has things changed again?" "No nothing has changed mother. We are still getting married, but we decided to go to the Justice of the Peace next month. We can have a ceremony down the line." "He sure is trying to come out cheap, aien't he? That boy just aien't got no class, does he?" "This was my idea, he wanted a big wedding but I said no." "Why would you do something stupid like that? I know why...because you ashamed of him aren't you? You don't want our snooty out of town relatives to come and see his no good behind." "No, that is not why and stop talking about Joe like that. I am just not into all that stuff for one day. I think it's a waste of money. If we are going to make things work, it will work with or without a big wedding." "You got that right, but I still want to be there."

"No problem I will let you know once we have decided on the exact date." "I guess that's fair then." "I love you momma and we'll see you next week." "You better believe it! A freight train couldn't stop me from coming to see my baby.

I love you honey and you take care now." "Good night momma." "Good night baby." Nina felt so much better after she talked to Denise and she decided to go in and check on Jeffrey and Jeanine. Nina stood at their bedroom doors and watched them as they slept. They were the perfect little pair. She felt Freddy walk up behind her and put his hands on her shoulders. "Honey, are you coming back to bed?" "Yes in a minute." "Are the kids sick?" "No they're fine." Freddy put his arms around Nina and held her close. "So what are you doing then?" "I'm just admiring my two little creations." (Freddy nestled his chin right by Nina's neck as he hugged her close from behind. He stood there in silence and watched the kids with her.) "They are wonderful kids, Nina. Once we get married can I adopt them? I want them to know they have a Daddy who cares; a man that won't run out on them and who loves them unconditionally." Nina turned around and buried her head in Freddy's chest as she hugged him close to her. "Please don't ever leave us." "I promise you I am not going anywhere."

They both walked back to their bedroom hand in hand like two school kids. "We better get some sleep we have a lot of planning and running around to do tomorrow to get our wedding set up." "You're right Freddy, good night." "Goodnight baby." When they got up the next morning they were headed off to the stores. Nina couldn't believe how much trouble planning a wedding could be. She had been out all week looking for decorations and getting a caterer. She was really ready to get this show on the road.

This evening they were going to Freddy's old church to ask Pastor Samuels if he would marry them. When it was just Nina and the kids her weekend work schedule never allowed them to go to church. She liked working on Sunday because she got paid double time and she needed the money back then. If she was off, most of the time Nina was too tired to get there or didn't feel like taking the bus. Freddy said he use to go all the time awhile back, but he had allowed his business to take up most of his time. As they walked in the church Nina started to feel a little uneasy. "Freddy, I feel a little strange about asking this man to marry us since neither one of us has been going to his church." "Don't worry about it…I'm sure he will understand. I was raised in this church and the man knows me." "Okay well you do all the talking because I don't know what to say."

Once they got in the church the secretary escorted them into the Pastor's office. As they entered the room, the Pastor got up and greeted them with open arms, "Brother Freddy how are you doing? It's been awhile now hasn't it?" "Yes Pastor it sure has this is my fiancé, Nina." "Sister Nina, welcome to our church home." "Thank you it's nice to be here." "Yes child it is always good to be in the house of the Lord. So I here you two are getting married. Congratulations!" "Thank you Pastor. We wanted to see if you would be available to marry us one Saturday this month. I know its short notice and it will be a small affair at my home. Nothing fancy…so whenever you are available, we can work around your schedule." "Am I available…son you better come here and give me another hug."

(The Pastor grabbed Freddy and gave him a big hug and then he grabbed Nina and hugged her too.) "Of course I am available. Bless your name Father for this union. You are a good man Freddy and God sees your goodness. I am always available for my flock. I watched you sing in the choir and usher here at church as a young boy. I also watched you grow up and be a successful business man. I knew God had his hand on your life. I knew you were going to be blessed. I'm going to say my peace because

I judge no man, that is God's job. But here it goes…Brother Freddy God needs his angel back on the front line. I know the Lord is still in your heart but what you got to remember, is that all that business you got going on aien't nothing without God. Brother Freddy do right by the Lord. Do right by this new union you are about to create. You are always welcome in the house of the Lord. Come as you are son. Make no mistake about it God will accept you, but you got to surrender yourself to him. As for me and my house, we will serve the Lord. What you going to do in your house Brother Freddy? Don't let the enemy have no play in your life, because every time you turn your back on God the enemy is waiting for you. Come on home Brother Freddy!"

Nina watched her soon to be husband slowly fall to the floor on his knees with his arms spread out as he looked towards the ceiling. Nina didn't know what was going on, so she got on her knees with him because she thought he was hurt or something. Then he started to shout, "Bless your name Father. Please forgive me Lord for I have sinned. Accept me back in your house. Please Lord, continue to love me. Don't turn away from me."

Freddy started to cry and Nina began to put her arms around him. Freddy held Nina back very tight. They were both down on their knees holding each other as the Pastor walked around them praising God. Nina thought it was almost like she could see the love in the room and she wanted to feel it too. Nina wanted to see what it was like to be in such a peace that your body goes limp. The Pastor embraced them both and said, "Now that the Holy Ghost has had his way, we thank you Father. I would like the two of you to go out and speak with my secretary Betsy, so she can set up your marriage counseling sessions. I think the two of you are meant for each other, so a few sessions should do it. Now, how about we plan on having the wedding on the last Saturday in the month?" "That's perfect Pastor, thank you so much." "I will see you in church this Sunday, won't I?" "Yes we will be there." "Sister Nina you have a good man here. Remember to put God first and your husband second and he will bless this union." "Yes Pastor I will."

Freddy took Nina's hand and they walked out into the hallway. "What just happened back there? You never told me you were some type of saint." "Baby it never came up. I am definitely not a saint. I use to really be into God and church and all that. But I started to focus my energy on my business and lost my focus on God. I knew I was wrong but I was so far from God I didn't know how to come back. I guess he has been in my heart all this time and Pastor just opened a door for him to shine his light through me." "What does that mean for us?" "Nothing has changed between us, we are still getting married. But we will have to stop fornicating, because it is wrong in the eyes of the Lord.

I know it is wrong for you to live with me as well, but I am not going to ask you and the kids to go anywhere. There are a lot of things I have to repent for so I will just include that on my list. Nina will you try and understand and accept the glory of God with me as I try to walk back in his ways?" "I want too…I want to know what it's like. I want to feel what you feel. I respect your beliefs and I will sleep in the guest room until we are married. I support you honey, I support you in everything you do. Will you show me how?" "Show you what, baby?" "Show me how to love the Lord, show me how to be saved. What do I have to do?" "First you have to repent and turn away from sin. You have to know in your heart that Jesus died for our sins. Why don't we come to church this Sunday and we will both learn to walk in his ways together?" "Okay we will." They finally walked over to the secretary as she greeted them with open arms. "God bless you Brother Freddy and God bless you sister. Marriage is a wonderful thing." (They both responded back in unison) "Yes it is!"

A few days had gone by and it was Sunday morning. As they got ready for church it was pouring down raining outside. "Freddy it is raining, are you sure you still want go?" "Of course I do. You think I am going to let a little rain stop me. I have made up my mind that God sent me to that church at that very time to show me he still loves me. He hasn't turned his back on me and I'm not about to turn my back on him again. The twins are already ready, so come on." Nina put on her light blue dress and slipped into her high heels and headed downstairs. When they got to the church it was packed. "I can't believe this, don't these people know it is pouring outside? I thought we would be the only fools out in this weather."

"Baby I told you when you are expecting God to show up nothing stops you. These are my folks and if Pastor still brings the Word like he use too, the place will be on fire." Nina just looked at her future husband as he pulled in front of the church. "Why are you pulling up here?" "So you and the kids can get out and I'll park the car." (Nina and the kids darted out the car and got inside the church lobby to wait for Freddy) Nina just looked around as she thought to herself that she planned to stay right by the door because she did not know these people and she wasn't trying to be left alone with them. Nina put her arms around the kids as they waited. An elderly lady walked up to them smiling, "Good afternoon sister." "Good afternoon." "What beautiful children you have." "Thank you." "Are you a new member?" "No we are just visiting today." "Well welcome to our church home. What church are you visiting from?" "Church...Ah no... we are not visiting from a church. We are just visiting... I mean we are looking for a church."

"God bless you sister, let the Lord lead you. I am Elder Stokes and I am head of the hospitality ministry so it's my job to make you feel right at home. You know we have a wonderful Bible study program for the children, would you like me to take them there?" "No thanks they will stay with me." Nina looked through the crowd and saw Freddy. She was so relieved that he was finally coming in the door. As Freddy walked towards Nina the elderly woman looked like she was in shock when she saw Freddy. "Brother Freddy!" "Mother Stokes, how have you been? It is good to be home." "We sure did miss you baby. I thought you left the area or had gone out of town on business. You just up and left Mother without a word."

"I know and I'm sorry I had some issues I needed to deal with." "Baby we all got issues, that's why we all need to be at the alter every Sunday. Don't you let no devil twist up your head. You take them issues to the Lord." "Yes mother I am. Have you met my fiance and her children?" "Fiance!" (Mother Stokes grabbed them up and hugged them so tight they couldn't breathe.) "Girl you been standing here looking like you some stranger, you family now. Yall go on upfront and get a seat." They made their way to the front of the church and there were four women and two men with microphones singing in harmony as they walked around the church. They were worshipping and praising God asking everyone, "Do you love the Lord today? I said do you love the Lord. Well if you really love him then everybody get up on your feet and make a joyful noise. We gonna praise him today so hard that we gonna rattle the gates of hell. Do I have some folks in here that just want to make the devil down right angry today? The whole congregation was on their feet shouting and screaming. Then the music came on and the women started to sing, "Halle…halle.. Hallelujah! The Lord is worthy to be praised…" Freddy took Nina's hand and she stood up with him and started to clap to the music.

The four women singing sounded like they should be on the radio, this was like a concert. The next song they sung was upbeat and the church had a dance they did to it. They all went from side to side clapping and shouting and turning around. Nina finally was able to keep up after Jeanine turned her body in the right direction. They were all up doing the dance singing about Jesus and Nina was having such a good time. Once everyone had settled down the Pastor came on and they all cheered.

Nina did not remember church being like this at all. She thought they acted like the Pastor was a celebrity or something. As the crowd settled down the Pastor walked up to the microphone and said, "Amen! Amen! Let the congregation say Amen! (Everyone shouted Amen back.) Now can I direct your attention to second Samuel chapter 24 verse 14? Can we talk about his mercy today?" Someone from the back of the church shouted, "Yes Pastor, preach!" Nina looked around as the people shouted back at the Pastor. "David said to Gad, I am in deep distress. Let us fall into the hands of the Lord for his mercy is great; but do not let me fall into the hands of men. That's a powerful scripture right there. Let me break this down to some of my new saints in here because I know my old saints got this thing down pat." One of the elderly members up front shouted back to the Pastor, "You right about it Pastor!" the Pastor just laughed and said, "Yeah right...keep your Bible's open. You all better listen up before you think you putting your trust in God and fall into the hands of man. Stop thinking you can do this by yourself. Who do you think woke you up this morning and got you on your way! Who do you think go that car financed that you driving in, when your cash was low and your credit couldn't get it! I'm talking about God! You better recognize his mercy! You better praise his name for being his child! (The congregation was on their feet shouting, stomping and screaming.) It's somebody out there right now that does not know his mercy. They think that man can solve all their problems. Do you know that man can walk out on you? Do you know once he is gone you might not find him again? I'm talking to some of my women out there.

You better stop worrying about who's sleeping in your bed and start worrying about who's gonna wake you up from that bed!" (The whole aisle that was in front of Nina went off. There were young women and two other women about her age jumping up and down. One of them ran around the church and a few of them started to jerk around and scream.) "I see God moving in this place!" Nina thought about the twin's father and how he just left her after she had them. After Nina delivered them in the hospital he came by to see if she was okay and she asked him to get her a snack from downstairs, he never returned. Nina believed he was going to marry her after the twins were born. Now she thought she had been a fool. A year later his brother contacted her and said he was killed by some girl's husband. Nina blocked that painful image out of her mind and focused back on the Pastor. She listened carefully as he said, "I know you are struggling with some issues right now but God will take you where you are! No man can do what God can do for you. I'm about to free up some souls today! The Pastor started to walk around the church laying his hands on people's forehead. Some people were shaking and some were falling out. Nina started to cry, she thought about all these years how it hurt her that this man, the father of her children, just walked out of the hospital without even saying goodbye.

She had struggled with this pain for so long that she wanted it to go away before she married Freddy. He didn't deserve to feel the pain she felt from her past. The Pastor walked up beside them and put his hands on their shoulders. He looked around the congregation and said, "I am about to marry this couple right here.

Praise you God for bringing this union together. No man shall separate this union. I said no man congregation! You see when God puts his hand on you nothing and nobody can remove it. I want to bless em today. The Lord has told me they need all the Holy Ghost power they can get in them because the devil is always trying to mess something up. He always got his hand in the pot trying to get his share. Brother Freddy don't you let no man tell you that you don't have time for God no more. See devil...you thought you had him. Ha hah, But I am going back out in the trenches and claiming some folks. I dare you to mess with my flock. Come on devil, try me...don't mess with my house!" The whole church was all over the place. People were laid out on the floor, in the pews, even the usher's were screaming and shouting. The Pastor pulled his oil out and rubbed it in his hand. He touched Nina's forehead and said, "No weapon that is formed against this child shall prosper. I am claiming her as an angel of God. She is part of my flock now and we will protect our sheep. Lord cover her with your blood." The last thing Nina heard the Pastor say was, cover her with your blood and she felt herself falling to the ground.

Nina felt a calm peace in her heart and she felt like she was being embraced. Once she came to, Freddy was fanning her and saying, "Thank you Father! Thank You Father!" Nina looked around for the kids but she didn't see them. "What happened? Where are the kids?" "They're fine baby they are in a room in the back with the other kids, they are just fine. Look at you, you are glowing. The glory of the Lord is upon you." At the end of service the Pastor asked if anyone wanted to give their life to Christ.

But Nina was too embarrassed to go up front and the Pastor must have been reading her mind. The Pastor looked around and said to his people, "Don't you have no fear of loving the Lord! You better get saved and save your household instead of worrying about what you gonna look like coming up here. I know one thing…I won't know what you look like in hell anyway. You better stop playing with your salvation and your kid's salvation." Nina got up and slowly walked to the front and Freddy followed her. "Well bless the Lord, sister." A few other women and two men came up front after her. Nina told the Pastor she wanted to have her and her children baptized. Then the whole congregation started screaming and shouting, the music started and everyone was all over the place again. After service was over on the ride home Freddy took Nina's hand and said now we are on one accord. For the first time in her life Nina felt like she could conquer the world. She felt strong in her spirit as if there wasn't anything she couldn't do. That was the greatest feeling she ever had.

Nina thought to herself, now she understand what it means to feel God's glory and she was so happy he allowed her to be touched by it. She planned on serving him forever. Nina couldn't wait until next Sunday for church. She wanted to get involved with the church and meet other women who were saved. Freddy could tell how excited she was as he pulled up to a bookstore. "What do you have to get from here?" "This is a Christian bookstore that used to get all my business. I figured since we are planning to begin our walk with the Lord together, we can all study together." "Study together? You mean you will read the Bible with me and help me understand it?" "Yes, sweetheart we can help each other understand it. We can get a Bible for the kid's that is on their reading level as well." "That sounds great, let's go!"

Chapter 10

Go After What You Want

Todd was taking on everything at school he had been working very hard and his hard work was paying off. He was at the top of his class and he had just been accepted into a highly sought after summer internship program. Todd sat at his desk as he thought about all that he had going on in his life. He had spoken to Lisa every night on the phone, and she was busy with her classes as well. He couldn't wait to see her again. All of a sudden one of his dorm buddies knocked on the door as he said, "Yo Todd! Yo Todd! Man you got a phone call." (Todd walked into the hallway to get the phone.) "Hello, this is Todd." "Hi dear how is class going?" "Hi Lisa things are going well, what about you?" "I have been so busy I never realized how much more you needed to know about God's word to preach it. I thought I knew that Bible, but boy am I learning some great stuff now."

"That's good baby, so you can teach me some more about the word when I get home, right?" "You got it Doctor!" Lisa and Todd had become really close but he knew that their marriage was going to be put on hold for a long time. The woman had a good head on her shoulders but he got the impression that after she finished Divinity School and her Master's Degree she was going for her doctorate and then she would probably be going after some other degree. That was all she talked about. He loved her so he figured he would just have to wait until she was ready. Todd was just asking God to guide him.

"Todd my class is going to a woman's retreat next weekend, so I won't be able to see you. I know I said I was going to come down there but this is a chance of a lifetime. I know it is going to be so awesome, can I go? Please!"

Lisa always did this to Todd. Once she got in school there was always something going on that put their relationship last on the list. Todd loved the Lord, but he knew that there had to be a balance. If there was not one would fail, either… her career, his career, or their marriage. At this point it seemed the marriage was never going to begin. Lisa was on point when it came to God, but she never even touched the surface in their relationship. This was the only weekend he had to see her before he did his internship and she knew it. "Sweetie I think the retreat sounds nice, but this will be our last weekend together before I leave. I don't know where I will be going yet. I am trying to get hooked up with Dr. Rutherford because he is one of the best doctors around. Honey this man travels everywhere so who knows where he will take me. I have to follow him so I can get underneath his wing. I really want him to be my mentor. I thought we talked about this already?" "I know and we did talk about it, but my retreat is important."

"So my career is not important?" "Todd I didn't mean to upset you and that is not what I meant. Of course your career is important. This internship does not judge what a good doctor you will be." "No you're right Lisa, it doesn't. But it does give me access to all the major players in the medical field. It also helps me determine exactly what type of medicine I would like to practice. It also allows me to get the inside track on all aspects of the medical field from every angle, not to mention the fact that this could help me get my foot in the door to open my own practice." "Yes that could or could not happen, you don't know this."

"I do know that every student who has participated in this program after finishing school has their own very successful practice. But I guess I will never know what I can do unless I try. Look Lisa I don't want to fight

I just want this weekend to be special, just the two of us." "I'm sorry we will have a lifetime for special weekends, but this weekend I will be at the retreat. I can make it up to you Todd, I have to go on this retreat, you don't understand. Do you realize how many other women here look up to me and are counting on me to be there? I am the star pupil in my class. Do you realize what it would look like if I didn't show up?" "It would look like you have a fiancé that you want to spend time with." "Are you asking me to choose between you and God?" "You know that I am not saying that. I support your efforts all the time, why can't you support mine. Just this once I need you to give something up for me." "I'm sorry Todd I cannot and I will not do that. I'll be at the retreat next weekend." (Lisa hung up the phone)

After Lisa hung up Todd got the feeling that this was what their marriage would be like. Whether he was a big time doctor or not, she would always try to be at the top of everybody's game no matter who she hurt in the process. He wanted a wife who stood by his side not in front of him. Todd planned on just letting go and letting God. He wasn't going to allow Lisa to put all her accomplishments before his or make him feel as though his were any less important anymore. If she was his soul mate then he knew eventually she would grow in the Lord pertaining to that area of her character and then they could be together.

But he was not going to sell his self short just because she appeared to be the perfect package to everyone else. Todd decided he was going to focus on his internship and if she was there when he was done, so be it. If not then maybe that was not God's plan for his life. He went back to his room and fell asleep and for some reason he had a dream about Denise.

Todd didn't know why she kept coming up in his spirit here lately. In his dream she was falling and he tried to run after her. He reached out his hand for her but he couldn't reach her. She just kept falling and then he woke up. When Todd got to class the next day he was waiting to hear what his assignment would be for his internship.

Todd's professor was very excited that he was accepted as he said, "Todd I was able to team you up with our dream team. You are my best student, so I am honored to put you amongst the best doctors in their field of medicine throughout the United States. Dr. Rutherford will head up your team." "Yes!" "I take it you know Dr. Rutherford?" "Yes sir I am very familiar with his work and his practice." "Good because he is a no nonsense type of guy and he will drill you in a heart beat. The man is a medicine genius, he knows his stuff. He hates to work around people who are incompetent, even students. That is why I am sending you because I know you will make me proud." "Thank you sir, so where will we be going?" "To the outskirts son, the hard knocks life area, the place where sickness knows sickness…" "So…professor you want to give me the city now or how about a state capital for a hint?" "Okay you pushed it out of me… the boogie down son, The Bronx." "New York!" "That's right son, the big apple."

Todd called his mother to let her know he would only be in New York, so he wasn't that far away. He thought about Denise again because he knew she was in that city, but he had no idea what part of New York or if she was still even staying there. Todd thought, who was he kidding there was no way he would run into Denise Combs in a big city like New York. Besides he would be so busy with this program he wouldn't have time for any social events. Todd started to get all his things organized and ready to pack, so it would all be done by the end of the week.

As the week went by Todd made sure that all his loose ends were tied up and his mom was all taken care of before his trip. The week actually went by pretty fast and it was time to start his journey with Dr. Rutherford. As Todd arrived to class the next day, he saw Dr. Rutherford writing his name on the chalkboard as he addressed the class, "I am Dr. Rutherford and I expect that you all should already know who I am. I think I need to remind you of just who you are dealing with. Research! Know your ailment and know how to cure it! That means you should know who is going to be a thorn in your side for the next few months and you should know how to ease the pain of pulling me out of your side. If I call on you and you can assist me and you know the proper procedures then I will slowly ease my thorn from your side. But if you are not prepared and I have to call on someone else in the group to answer a question for you, I will turn and twist that thorn until the pain is unbearable. You got that, rookies!

The class all said "Yes Dr. Rutherford!" "We are in the business of saving lives, that means there is no room for error and second guessing yourself. Do I make myself clear?" They all said, "Yes sir!"

There were three students selected by the Dean to work with Dr. Rutherford. Todd knew he was tough but he was ready for him. Todd also knew he was the best doctor in his field and that is why he wanted him as his mentor. Dr. Rutherford continued to drill them, "You all think you are hot shots because you want to be doctors. You think living the life of a doctor is big pay and fast cars? Well, let me tell you one thing it is long hours, hard work and dedication. Forget about what you heard because I am about to show you the raw and uncut version of being a doctor. We are headed to the Bronx, and you will see some wild stuff. So saddle up cowboys and put your tough hats on because we're about to take a ride, class is dismissed go get some rest you will need it. (They all hurried out of the classroom.) Once they got to the hotel and got settled in they decided to go play a little golf to relax. They figured this might be their last time to have any fun because they knew over the next few months they would be working like crazy. Most of the clinics in New York were short of doctors so they were kind of getting thrown in the line of fire as they learned.

As Todd positioned himself with his golf club, Dr. Rutherford walked onto the golf course and gave the students a smile. "Well boys it looks like you are developing my habits already. A good round of golf always gets me geared up for the next day. You mind if I join you?" The guys all looked scared and said, "Sure go right ahead." Todd knew that Dr. Rutherford was not the tough guy he played out to be. He was just simply preparing them for the worst and trying to toughen them up. Todd had been following Dr. Rutherford's work for quite some time, he even did a school paper on his practice.

All the man's patients praised him and said he was the nicest person on earth. They said he bent over backwards for them, even making house calls. His receptionist said he was the pillar of his community and he had the biggest heart you had ever seen. She also said when it came down to medicine and his practice everything had to be perfect and he spared no expense and he expected for them to have that same attitude. Dr. Rutherford looked at Todd and said, "Well son you gonna play or just stand there day dreaming?" "Sure I'll play you in a round of golf." No one knew that

Todd was a golf fanatic and he knew the game inside out. Todd turned up his skills and beat Dr. Rutherford several times. The other guys were too scared to beat him so they just watched. Dr. Rutherford was impressed that Todd didn't hold back. "I like that confidence, keep it up. You'll need it if you want to play in the big leagues. Now let's up our game. Before you take a swing I want you to answer whatever medical question I throw at you. If you can't answer it, you forfeit your turn"

"Okay that's fair let's go." Dr. Rutherford asked Todd about medical terms, terminology, what to do in certain procedures, how to handle different situations, etc. All the questions were extremely tough and the other guys didn't know most of the answers. Dr. Rutherford was banking on Todd not knowing the answers either. Little did he know that Todd had almost memorized his medical books. This was his calling and he had really put his heart into it. After Todd won each round, Dr. Rutherford smiled at him and said, "You did good…real good. Then he walked off the golf course and got into his S500 Mercedes and drove off.

Todd thought to himself, Dr. Rutherford was lifting the thorn in his side. As he walked off the golf course Todd exhaled as he watched him drive off. Todd was so glad that he knew the answers to all those questions. The other guys were amazed at Todd's knowledge as they walked up and shook his hand, "Man…how did you remember all that stuff?" "I don't know I guess my brain had just stored it up for a day like today." "Well whatever your brain did was impressive. But now we better head to our hotel to get some sleep before all our brains are fried in the morning."

When they got back to the hotel they were all exhausted and fell asleep quickly. At 5am they heard someone coming through their hotel door, "Okay you preschool doctors it is time to show me what you got." Dr. Rutherford was screaming to the top of his lungs at them. They all got up and got dressed. After they ate breakfast they headed to County Medical and went straight to the ER. They watched Dr. Rutherford assist with patching people up to doing heart surgery on an old woman, the man was amazing. Everyone in the center wanted his medical opinion. At first Todd had decided he wanted to be a Pediatrician, but he wanted to explore other areas of medicine before he made his final decision. This internship was designed to help young students get a first hand look at the different medical fields and everything that it entailed from a hands on perspective.

One day they would go with Dr. Rutherford, who was a heart surgeon. The next day they would go somewhere with Dr. Pow, who was a Plastic surgeon. Or they would go with Dr. Smith who was a Pediatrician. One weekend they went to an ER and hung out with the doctor's there. There was action all the time.

Todd was fascinated by all of their professions. He had learned so much from them these past few weeks that he had just blessed the Lord every night for putting him under such wonderful doctors. After a long hard day of work, Dr. Rutherford came into their rooms with a concerned look on his face and said, "We have a clinic that is having a flu epidemic and they need some doctor's to help out. My good friend Dr. Ruddy runs the clinic, so I told him we would come and give him a hand. We are going to drive down there tomorrow. It's Valley Turn Clinic and they are extremely overloaded.

I just want to warn you, that it will be very crowded and I am going to need you to be focused. People get ready to roll up your sleeves tomorrow because I have a feeling this is going to be hands on training for you guys. Get some rest!" As the guys looked at each other, one of them said, "Is he saying we are going to have to give flu shots?" Todd just shook his head and said, "Of course we are and maybe some other stuff. Isn't this what you came here for?" "Well yeah, but are you really ready to be dealing with a whole bunch of sick people in chaos trying to give your first flu shot?" "Now that you put it that way...I don't know. But what I do know is that I can do all things through Christ and he shall prepare me and give me the proper judgment to do what I am asked to do. Now good night gentlemen it looks like tomorrow will be a full day." "Yeah you're right man we have nothing to worry about... good night."

Chapter 11

Angels Are Watching Over You

Denise was so excited about the thought of becoming a nurse. The more she learned from the other nurses, the more she knew this was what she wanted to do. As Denise walked around her tiny apartment she began to straighten up and think to herself. She was so glad that her friend Leah, from her nursing school decided to come and study with her. She was the only real friend Denise had since she moved to New York. Leah had been so nice to her when she got here and she was very helpful. Joe had to work late at "Doonsberry's" tonight, so Leah and Denise had decided to study at her place tonight. Joe always volunteered to work late on Friday nights. He said since that was their busiest night the tips were bigger.

Denise was glad he would be gone so that they could have some peace and quiet while they studied. Things between Denise and Joe had been a little strange since he tried to rape her. Even though he had been jumping through hoops to make it up to her, she just didn't feel the same about him. They had made several attempts to go to the Justice of Peace to get married, but something always seemed to stop them. One time they got into a big argument on the way and decided to turn back around. Just last week Denise was supposed to meet him there but she got busy at work. By the time she got there they had closed and Joe was raging mad at her.

Denise recalled him choking her and grabbing her arm one time because her instructor called the house to see how she was doing? She had the flu the week before and she had fallen behind, so he just wanted to make sure that she would be able to keep up with class. Joe insisted that they must be having an affair and the reason why she couldn't sleep with him was because she was giving it up to her teacher.

When Denise told him he was a fool, he grabbed her and to say the least it was an ugly fight. She knew that Joe was a borderline abusive person, but somehow she thought she could change him. Denise knew he was frustrated because they weren't intimate. She thought once they got married and had a sexual relationship all this anger he had inside of him would subside. She felt like she just needed to be more patient with him. (As Denise heard knocking at the door, her thoughts were interrupted so she got up to answer the door.) "Leah! What's up girl?" "Nothing but exams girlfriend. Are you ready to do some serious studying tonight?" "You better believe it. I just put the coffee on and I made some snacks for us, do you want to eat first?" "Yes girl I am starving." Leah was a beautiful brown skin girl who had been married for two years and she seemed to be very happy. Her and her husband had just bought a house in New York. He was a lawyer and they both seemed to love each other very much. Denise always told her how lucky she was. Leah was a very reserved person she was quiet and never involved herself into the class gossip. She pretty much stayed focused on her learning. Denise really didn't know that much about her outside of the basic stuff they talked about in class.

Leah looked around the apartment and said, "Denise I like what you have done with this apartment. I don't recall these apartments being this nice." "They aren't, I had to do a major overhaul when we got here. With some paint and decorations I think it turned out okay. I hope me and Joe are able to purchase a home together after we get married." "First you have to get married and Denise just because you own a house it doesn't make it a home." "You got that right!

I suppose we will give it another shot at getting married next week." "You don't just suppose you will get married, what kind of response is that? You sure don't sound like a bride to be to me, so what is really going on girl?" "Well every time we go to the Justice of the Peace something happens, it never seems to fail." "Maybe that is God's way of telling you he doesn't approve." "I wouldn't know, me and God haven't been on speaking terms." "You're not saved Denise?" "No I don't think so, why is there a problem?" "Denise…as far as being my friend, no there isn't. I'm gonna love you like a sister regardless of your salvation because that is the right thing to do in the eyes of the Lord. As for your salvation, there is a problem. What type of friend would I be to not share the joy of Jesus Christ with you? Honey, hell is not a good place and I am about saving anybody from going there if I can help it."

"I thought I was already in hell." (Leah gave Denise a puzzled look) "What is that suppose to mean?" "I just feel like I came to New York for nothing, I feel hopeless and useless. I can't let my mother know I failed. I can't let her know that Joe stays out almost every night doing God knows what. When I do see him it is very brief. If we are together for a long period of time we end up arguing. I told him I planned on remaining a virgin until after we were married. At first he was cool with it, but after we moved in one time he tried to rape me. He accused me of sleeping with our instructor and then he hit me. (Denise started to cry heavy sobs)" She tried to pull herself together as she said, "Leah I didn't mean to drop all this on you. I guess it was just bottled up inside and I don't have anyone else to talk to, I am so sorry."

Leah sat there and looked at Denise with an expressionless face and then she walked over to her as she touched her shoulder she said, "What are you doing to change the situation?" "What do you mean, what am I doing? Joe would kill me if I tried to leave him. Plus I do love him, but things are just rocky right now, maybe we need counseling." "Denise you do need counseling. You need to ask yourself why a pretty intelligent young girl like yourself is allowing herself to be treated like this. It is up to you to take control of your life and your salvation. We are adults and we are held accountable for our own actions. You can't save the world, but you have the power to rescue Denise."

As Denise thought about what Leah said, she thought she made some very good points. She had lost herself in this relationship and she did have the power to control her own life. Leah walked over to the couch and got her purse, she pulled out a small black book. When Denise saw the title it said NIV Study Bible. Leah opened the book and started to read to Denise about the love of God. Then she got down on her knees and prayed for her. Leah pulled Denise by the hand to get on the floor with her and before she knew it she was praying as well. For the first time Denise felt like there was some hope behind her prayers for her circumstances.

After they finished praying Leah looked her in the eyes and said, "Denise I do not judge anyone it is your choice to come to Christ. All I can do is, invite you to fellowship with me in church sometimes, would you like to do that?" "Yes I would. My mother recently got saved and I promised her I would find a church in New York, but I don't know the area that well yet."

"Well now you know someone who can show you the ropes, I will even come pick you up. Now we better hit the books. After they ate their sandwiches they opened their books and started to quiz each other on the terms they had to memorize. The whole time they were studying Denise had hoped Leah would not look at her differently now that she knew her situation. Denise thought she wouldn't blame Leah for leaving after she told her she was an abused nut basket. But Denise felt better after she shared her pain with Leah. It had been so bottled up inside her that she needed to tell someone. It was nice to have a shoulder to cry on. For the first time Denise felt like she had a true girlfriend.

After a long night of intensive studying they both looked up as Joe walked in the front door. "You girl's still at it? Do you know it's three in the morning?" "Yes we know we are almost finished...Oh honey this is my friend Leah" (Leah got up to shake Joe's hand) "Hi Joe, nice to meet you." "You too." Joe walked back in the bedroom and turned the TV on. Denise could tell that Leah felt a little uncomfortable as she was packing up her books and said, "Well it is very late and I think we just about covered everything. So Denise, do you think you're ready for an A?" "Girl I hope so, I sure appreciate all your help. Please tell your husband that I am sorry I kept you out so late."

"He's fine, I told him we were pulling an all nighter. Remember he went to law school, he knows how killer exams can be." "Leah thanks for listening to me I am sorry I came off like a stupid abused bimbo or something." "First of all you did not come of like a stupid abused bimbo.

You have to stop putting yourself in those categories. Don't worry God will guide your heart. You need to get yourself around some praying folk's girl." (They both started to laugh) "You must be right." "I cannot believe you haven't had any saved friends in high school." "Actually I had one, his name was Todd and we went on a date to church once." "Oh well I like him already, what happened to him?" "I picked Joe instead and I brushed him off. I just thought I could never be on his level. Every time I was around him I felt like he was a saint and I was a sinner.

"Did he say that to you or make you feel that way?" "Who, Todd? Oh no he was a perfect angel. He worshipped the ground I walked on, that was just how I made myself feel. If I had to do it all over again I would have chosen him because he was a gentle spirit. I always thought I liked the rough guy type or the image of a rough guy. But nobody likes being ruffed up." "Girl hang in there, I will continue to pray for you. You have to make this decision on your own whether to leave or to stay. But if you need a place to stay you can always have my guest room. Denise, don't hesitate to call me if you need help and I don't care what time it is…Denise I mean it. You are my sister now and I am here for you. But most of all God is here for you. You can call on him when you need him. I know you are standing in the midst of a storm right now, but he can pull you out. Look to God, he won't let you down. (Leah reached in her purse and pulled out the little black Bible) "Here take this." Leah turned around and walked down the hallway as Denise closed the door she heard Joe walk up behind her. "Hey!" "Hey honey you scared me, I thought you were sleep." "What was that all about?" "What are you talking about?" "You know what I am talking about.

I heard you tell your little girlfriend you are in trouble with me." "Joe that is not what I meant! I can't believe you were ease dropping on me." "What are you trying to get me in some type of trouble or something?" (Joe looked down at the Bible that was in Denise's hand) "What is that?" "Oh this…Leah gave me the Bible to read." "Now you think reading the Bible is going to save you?" "No Joe…that is not what I think. Look it's late and we are both tired so I'm going to bed." Denise really was not in the mood to fight with Joe so she walked away from him and began to pick up the dishes they had in the living room to put into the kitchen sink. As she put the dishes in the sink, Joe cornered her and grabbed both her arms. "Joe you promised you would never hurt me again." "Oh yeah…well you promised you would stand by me and support me. I wouldn't call you down talking me to your little uppity girlfriend supporting me. Do you know I will kill you up in here girl?" They began to struggle as she tried to loosen his grip on her arms.

Denise was kicking and yanking Joe's arms away uncontrollably and then she felt a sharp pain coming from her head. All of a sudden blood was rushing down her face. Joe had punched her above her forehead and she felt like she wanted to faint. She screamed out, "God help me!" "God can't help you now. This is between me and you." Denise reached over and grabbed the hot coffee pot that was on the stove and threw it on Joe. "Aaaghh! I'm gonna kill you." As Joe raced towards her she managed to get out of the front door. Joe was running behind her and he was fast on her trail. Denise knew she was going to die this morning, but she was going out with a fight. She started to knock on people's doors begging for help.

Then a man wearing a t-shirt and boxer shorts came out of his door and said, "What is going on out here! I don't tolerate no domestic violence in my building!" The man stood in front of Joe and said, "You can try me if you want son, but I guarantee you will loose." "Oh yeah you think so, get out of my way old man." "Sorry I can't do that." "Why not, this is not your problem." "Yeah well you made it my problem and I think you better go on upstairs for I introduce you to my partner." "What partner?" "My sawed off shot gun." (The man reached inside the door of his apartment and pulled out a long back shot gun. Then Joe took off running up the stairs) Denise had finally made it outside as she walked around she realized she had nowhere to go. She was starting to feel faint so she walked over to the curb and sat down. She started to talk to herself, "What am I going to do, I couldn't grab my purse, I have no car keys and no money. The only friend I have in this town is Leah. But I don't want to tell her what Joe did." After she walked around for an hour she figured that Leah was her only hope, but she needed to find some change to call her.

Denise remembered how Leah said call on the Lord so she decided to give it a try. "Lord if you are watching, help me please! I need you Lord! Where are you?" (People started to stare at Denise as they walked by) As she looked back at them she realized they were on the curb and she was in the middle of the street in New York screaming to the Lord at four o' clock in the morning and everyone thought she was stoned or crazy. She didn't even care, she just held her face down and began to cry. "Why! Why!"

Denise put her hand on the ground to level herself so she could get up and there it was. There was a quarter lying right there on the ground under her hand. "Thank You Lord! Thank You Lord!" She ran over to the payphone and called Leah. "Can I please speak to Leah." "She's sleep, who's calling?" "I know you don't know me but I am her friend from class that she study's with. I really need her help, can you please wake her up?" "Can't this school stuff wait until tomorrow? She just got in and she is really tired." Tears began to stream down Denise's face and she decided to say a silent prayer. "Lord, please help him understand without me having to explain my situation to him. I am so embarrassed and the last thing I need is a man's opinion about my situation." Her prayer was interrupted by Leah's husband, "Hello, are you still there?"

"Look I can't wait!" Denise heard Leah in the background say, "Who is it honey?" "The girl you study with." "Denise? Give me the phone. Denise is that you?" "Yes" "What's wrong?" "Leah he beat me up, he heard our whole conversation. I had to run out of the house without my car keys or my purse. I am on 26th street and all I have are the clothes on my back. I hate to get you involved, but I don't have anyone else to call. Please help me!" "I'm on my way, just stay put."

Denise sat on a park bench and waited for Leah. She looked around and saw all kinds of people walking the streets. Then she noticed there was a church across the street. The sign on the basement door read "Shelter for Women" she wanted to go in and see what the shelter was like. She thought maybe they could help her find a place to live. She didn't want to be a burden on Leah and her husband.

Denise knew she couldn't call her mother for help because she knew if she found out what happened, her and Freddy would end up in jail after they killed Joe. Once she got into the church she walked down into the basement where the sign pointed. As soon as she got inside a woman walked up to her and said, "Do you need help?" "I don't know…my boyfriend beat me up and I ran out. I saw the sign so I wanted to get some more information." "Do you need medical assistance?" "No! It's just a little bruise, the bleeding has stopped." "Have you reported this attack to the police?" "No!" "Then what would you like for us to do for you, it sounds like you have everything under control?" (Denise was outraged at the women's disregard for her situation.) "Look I suppose you can't do anything" As Denise started to walk away she heard the woman mumble to herself, "Lord help her." "What did you say?" "I asked the Lord to help you." "Help me? It sounds like you are the one who needs help with her attitude. I thought this place was here to help people?" "I am here to help people that are trying to get out of their situations. But you are a victim who apparently wants to remain a victim."

"What gave you that idea?" "Because somebody just whipped your behind and you don't plan to do anything about it. You were fortunate enough to walk out of the situation. There are thousands of women who have to be carried out…that is in a body bag." "Look he was just upset, plus I said some bad things about him…he was angry, that's all. I never said I planned on going back." "I heard it all before, honey. Until you decide to get angry and stop making excuses for his one two punches, nothing will change." "Didn't I just say I was through with him!"

"Mmmh…well only you know that… look sweety, what do you want to do because I have to take a few ladies down to the chapel for our morning prayer?" "Can I come?" "Sure you can come." Denise followed the woman and three other ladies down to the chapel. Once they got there they all kneeled down to pray. The woman kneeled down beside Denise and held her hand. As they prayed together she could feel a lifting in her spirit. The more Denise called out to God the more she felt this heavy weight being slowly removed from her body. Once they were done the woman helped her to get up. "Well baby girl I think you're ready." "Ready for what?" "Ready to loose that zero who whipped your butt." "Yes maam I am!"

"Good I'm glad to hear that. Now you can stay here if you like, but I still think you need to see a doctor about those bruises." Denise remembered that she had asked Leah to pick her up. "Oh my goodness, I forgot that I called my friend to pick me up, I have to go." Denise raced out the front door and across the street. She looked all over the place for Leah but she didn't see her. All of sudden Denise heard someone calling her name, "Denise! Denise!" "Here I am Leah!" Leah and her husband ran towards Denise and Leah wrapped her arms around her. When Leah saw that Denise had dry blood in her hair, she started crying. "It's really not that bad." "You are coming to live with us. We have a bedroom in our basement and it's yours at no charge. We just want you to be safe." Leah's husband looked at Denise and said, "That's right our home is your home, God bless you sister. The Lord will go out before you and fight this battle because your victory is already won.

Don't you worry about a thing we are going to help you get through this." Leah's husband, Bradley rubbed Denise's back and helped her into his SUV. When they got to their house Denise was impressed at how nice the neighborhood was. This was nothing like where she lived. They had a three bedroom home that was very cozy. Their basement had a bathroom and a family room up front. They had decorated it very nice and it was fully furnished. She thought this was so much nicer than their little apartment the only thing that was missing was a kitchen.

Leah brought Denise some bandages and some pajama's. "Let me clean those nasty wounds for you." "You don't have to do that Leah. Please tell your husband thank you for letting me stay, you both have been great. But I can't impose on you like this. I will just stay the night and go home in the morning." "Go home to what Denise, a man who beats you for telling the truth? You deserve better than this." "I know and I plan to have better than this. I went to the chapel and prayed to God before you guys got there, that is where I was when you were looking for me. I have decided that it is time for me to give my life to Christ. I don't want to live like this anymore. As I prayed I could feel angels hovering over me. I just know that they protected me tonight.

God had to reveal Joe's evil spirit to me Leah. He had given me so many signs and I chose to ignore them. But I guess I couldn't ignore this one could I? I owe my life to God and if I don't turn this situation around for his glory and serve him then I am useless." Leah grabbed Denise and hugged her and they both started to cry again.

They both held hands and praised God as they thanked him for his deliverance and security. Leah helped Denise clean the blood from her face and bandage her wounds. Denise decided to call in for work the next day because she looked like she had been in a dog fight. She decided since she had the day off she could look for an apartment of her own. Once she got the newspaper she started to begin her search. Things were looking up and God was looking down on her. After apartment hunting all day, Denise had found three places in her price range. Of course they were all very small, but she knew she would make it work. Denise knew Joe would be at work so she went by the apartment and got all her stuff. She decided to leave him a note that said, "I can't do this anymore. My spirit and well being is worth so much more than you would ever be willing to give. Therefore I release you from my life and I wish you well."

When Joe got home from work and read the note, he just tore it up and said, "Yeah whatever." As he threw the note in the trash the phone rang, "Hello I'm trying to reach Denise Combs." "She doesn't live here anymore." "Well is this her fiancé, Joe?" "Who's asking?" "Yes…my name is Trudy, I am one of the nurses at the clinic. I know she called in sick today, but I wanted to let her know we are having a clinical study this evening that I knew she wouldn't want to miss." "Lady didn't I say she don't live here anymore." (Joe slams the phone down) "Let's see how Denise gets along in the big city without me. I'm glad she came to get her stuff, since Claire is going to move in with me next month anyway. So…Little Ms. Virgin can go ahead about her business. I'm about to have me a real woman and as much loving as I want.

Denise will probably come running back here asking me to take her back, once she finds out that Claire is my girl now." Meanwhile Denise thought her apartment hunting had gone well. When she told Leah about the apartment prospects she had, Leah and Bradley both said that Denise should stay there. Leah explained to Denise that all those areas were high in crime and that was no place for a single women to be alone, especially with the late hours she worked. Leah and her husband both agreed Denise would be much safer in their basement. Denise also realized that their basement was bigger than all the apartments she had looked at. She went and hugged them both and said, "I can't repay you for what a blessing you are to me." Leah said, "The good news is you don't have to repay us, we are glad we were here for you."

Once Denise put away all her things she decided to call the clinic to let them know what was going on. As soon as someone picked up the phone she recognized the voice, "Thank You for call."(Trudy is interrupted) "Hey Trudy it's me." "Denise?" "Yep, what's up?" "What is going on baby, I was worried about you. You never call in sick and you know that clinical study that you have been waiting for is tonight." "Tonight, oh no with all the excitement I forgot." "What excitement? Why did Joe say you didn't live there and he was very rude on the phone, what happened?" (Trudy was like a hen mother and she treated them all like her daughter's. After Denise told her what happened, Trudy was ready to go over there herself and kick Joe's butt.) "Baby, don't you worry about a thing. You take as much time as you need to and your job will be right here." "Thanks so much for being so understanding. I will be back in the swing of things in a couple of days.

When Denise got off the phone she praised God for allowing her to keep her job and for working for such a great group of people. After a few days she was ready to get back to work. When she walked in, the place was crowded and it was jammed pack with sick people coughing, sneezing, and wearing mask. One of the nurses looked over at her and said, "Denise you're back!" Then everyone came over and gave her a big hug. They all said how sorry they were about what happened. Denise didn't mind that Trudy had told all of them her story, because she felt like she needed their support anyway. They all started to treat her like she was a child or something. One of the nurses brought her a cup of tea and the other one helped her to a seat. Then Trudy walked in with a bag full of brochures about domestic violence.

Denise appreciated the attention but this was going way too far, "Look everybody I'm fine. Now we have a lot of sick people out there, so can I just get to work?" Trudy looked at Denise and said, "Honey that filing is going to have to wait. We need everybody to pitch in and help us out. You can make sure everyone has signed in first. Then give them the paperwork, remember to look over it once they are done. Just make sure everything is filled out. If it doesn't apply to them, then put N/A in the box. Please make sure you check all insurance cards. As they leave see if they need another appointment and just put it in the schedule book. I will show you how to use the computer to key in appointments later."

(Denise was so excited that she was stepping up from filing even if it was just for a day.) "Yes Trudy, no problem." Denise ran to the front desk and she was determined to make a good impression on Trudy.

Denise thought if she did a good job, maybe Trudy would consider her for a promotion. She got the desk organized as the people started to swarm in the clinic like bees. She couldn't believe this bug had all these people sick. Denise noticed a distinguished gentleman walk in the clinic that did not look sick at all as she said, "How can I help you sir?" "Hi young lady I'm Dr. Rutherford and I'm here to see Dr. Ruddy." "He is with a patient right now. You can have a seat and I'll let him know you are waiting." (As Denise motioned the man to the waiting area, Trudy walked out of the back room and ran over to the man.) "Dr. Rutherford, I am so glad you could come. It is an honor to have you here. Why are you in the waiting room, we need you back here?" (Dr. Rutherford didn't say a word he just followed Trudy to the back.) As Denise watched Dr. Rutherford walk towards the back she began to help another patient with his paperwork. Five other doctors walked in the front door and Trudy showed them to the back

Trudy walked up to Denise and said, "Do you have any idea who that is?" "Who are you talking about?" "That man that I just escorted to the back is the famous and very handsome Dr. Rutherford. He is training some students and they are back there now helping out. I am so glad he could come to give us a hand. By the way I saw a cute one back there for you." "The last thing I'm thinking about is a man right now, Trudy." "Don't you let a good man pass you by because another one was a snake." "I won't Trudy, but I need to regroup right now." Denise got up and walked to the back to post a patient's chart on the back of the door and she bumped into one of the doctor's.

"Oh excuse me. I'm sorry it's just so crowded in here." "No problem sister." Denise turned around when she recognized the voice. "Todd!" "Denise!" They ran into each other's arms and held each other tight. Todd touched her face as he noticed the bruises, "What happened?" "This is nothing, so you're a doctor already?" "No, I'm just on an internship I'm working under Dr. Rutherford. Why is your face bruised, did someone attack you?" "It's a long story." "Can we talk about it over dinner tonight?" "Yes I would like that."

By the time they got out of the clinic it was late and Todd waited for Denise outside. As she walked up to Todd's car he said, "Why don't you leave your car here and ride with me. I will bring you back to pick it up." "Okay sure." Todd walked around and opened the passenger door for Denise. When she got into the car Todd looked over at her. "You have been on my mind and in my spirit ever since I got here. I kept having this dream of you falling and I couldn't catch you. God was trying to tell me that you needed me. Denise you have been in my heart for so long. I got engaged to Lisa because I thought she was the ideal wife for a man of God. I was so busy trying to live up to a holy image that I forgot to follow my heart.

I wanted to stop you the day I saw you walk off that graduation stage. I wanted you to know that I loved you. But I knew I wanted my wife to be saved and when Lisa came along she seemed like the perfect woman. But she hasn't even called me to see how I was doing, since I left. She is so caught up in her own life that she doesn't have time to care about me or what is going on with my life. I didn't realize that until after our relationship had really gotten serious.

Yes, Lisa does love the Lord but she doesn't love me, not like I need a wife to love me and support me." "Todd... I love the Lord too." "What do you mean?" "I mean I have gotten saved while I was here in New York. I have given my life to Christ and I am serving him. I attend church on the west side with my friend Leah every Sunday. We also go to Bible study together. Last Sunday I joined our dance ministry. When I saw them perform I knew I had to be up there. Todd you won't believe this, but I actually read the Bible now, I can't believe those Israelites. My favorite is the Book of Ruth. (Todd just sat there and looked at her in amazement with her beauty and new found passion for the Bible.)

When Denise noticed Todd staring at her she said, "What?" He leaned over and kissed her gently on the lips and said, "You are my angel. God doesn't always send us gifts dressed up in the packages that we think they should be. Sometimes we have to let go and let God do his work. Once he shows us what's in our heart we need to follow it. Never transform yourself to do what people think you should do or be. Never put your trust in man." Denise loved Todd as well and everything he said hit home. She knew at that moment she could spend the rest of her life with him. She leaned over and kissed him back and they headed down the road for dinner.

During their car ride, they talked about everything. They filled each other in on what was happening in their lives. Denise also told him about what happened with Joe. They both agreed things happened for a reason.

Chapter 12

After The Storm: Keep Standing

Todd and Denise had become very close. They had been dating for three years now and life was good. After that dinner from the night he ran into her at the clinic, Todd had told Claire that he thought it was best to call off their engagement. Claire actually agreed with him, she said that school was more important. She also told him that she had decided that marriage and children would get in her way of trying to achieve her goals. The last thing anyone had heard about Claire was that a church in Dallas, Texas was considering her as being a co-pastor. Denise's entire family was now a praying family and it was so nice. As they say a family that prays together stays together. The Lord was just opening so many doors for Denise and Todd. Their friendship had evolved into a loving relationship. They were about to complete school and they had been planning their wedding for eight months now. Denise couldn't believe the day was finally here. Her mom had made all the arrangements and it was going to be a lavish affair.

Nina was right there by Denise's side helping her get ready for her wedding. "Sweet pea you look absolutely breathe taking. The Lord has been so good to us." "He certainly has mama." As her mother helped her with her makeup, Todd's mother walked in. "Look at my daughter-in-law, isn't she beautiful?" Todd's mother came over and gave Denise a hug and then she hugged Nina. Since Todd and Denise had been together his mother and Nina had become the best of friends. It was an awesome wonder to love the Lord, but it was even more awesome to be surrounded by people with like minds. Both of their mothers started praying and praising God and Denise joined in with them. Denise smiled as she thought this was such a wonderful day.

After Todd and Denise were married, they were picked up by a limousine. It took them to the airport to start their honeymoon. They decided to go to Hawaii. Once they got in the limo, they were all over each other. Todd pulled Denise next to him and said, "We're married now I can give you a real kiss." They kissed so much on the ride to the airport that her lips hurt. They both slept on the airplane. When they got to the room it was laid out. Todd made all the honeymoon plans. Denise figured he probably used all his savings for this trip. She told him several times she didn't need a fancy honeymoon. She thought they should save the money for a house. But he insisted he was going to pay for everything. Denise knew that medical school was expensive and they needed to start saving until they got better jobs.

As Denise looked around she said, "Baby this place is amazing but this must have cost a fortune. Can we afford this? I said I wanted to go to Hawaii, but we do have to eat this week." "So you think I would let my bride starve in this beautiful room. You just relax, don't you worry about a thing. I spare no expense when it comes to my wife." "You are too good to me. But I'm serious Todd we need to save every penny because my man is about to become a doctor. I have already thought about this and I will get two jobs to help put you through the remainder of medical school. We are in this together baby."

"That's why you're my wife because you always have my back. But you're a millionaire so you don't need to work any job if you don't want too." "I know I am rich in the eyes of the Lord but God also said don't be no fool.

I am going to call the front desk to see if we can switch our room. Maybe they have something cheaper. This is too much…we definitely don't need the penthouse suite." "I'm serious Denise, you are a millionaire." Denise had already picked up the phone to call the front desk. She couldn't believe how upscale this place was. Even the phone was incased in gold. Todd walked over to her and took the phone and placed it back on the receiver. Denise looked at him and said, "What are you doing?" "There is something I need to tell you. When my father died he was a very wealthy man. He left me and my mother four million dollars each and the family business. His plumbing business alone makes more money than me and my mother could ever spend. Plus I have made some other investments that have been very lucrative. So when I say you're a millionaire I mean it, I mean we are millionaires." Denise looked at Todd in amazement. "Are you serious?" "Yes baby I am. You can have whatever you want." "Then if you have all this money why don't you and your mom buy some big house. Why haven't you bought a BMW or a Mercedes. I mean doesn't every millionaire at least have one luxury car.

"Denise we don't care about that materialistic stuff. My mom wanted to stay in that house because she said it had a lot of memories of my Dad. I never wanted to drive to school in a luxury car anyway, besides don't you think I got enough attention? We give a lot of money to the church and different charities. We also support local community programs, but we like to keep a low profile. All the recognition belongs to God." Denise just sat there in awe of her husband as she said, "I was right…you are an angel."

Denise started to kiss Todd as she started to undress him. After they made love they were like two school kids. They had formed a bond that was so strong she got butterflies in her stomach every time she looked at him. During their honeymoon they talked about opening a Family Clinic in Philly and buying a house close to their families. Denise walked over to Todd and sat on his lap while he was watching the world news.

"There is a ten car accident on the freeway in Philly. I am trying to get the full story." "You know some fool is always backing up traffic. Let's go take a walk on the beach." Denise grabbed Todd by the hand to get up from the couch. Then they got dressed and headed to the beach. They walked hand in hand along the shore and talked about all the things they were going to do when they got home.

They wanted to have the biggest family practice in Philly and Denise wanted her mother to be the manager. She couldn't wait to get home to tell her that they were millionaires. As she looked at Todd she realized that everything she went through was worth it just to have this very moment. They got to the lobby and Todd took her in his arms as they danced all the way to their suite. Todd looked Denise in her eyes and said, "I love you so much." "I love you to husband." They danced over to the bed and started to undress each other and then Denise saw the blinking red light on the phone. "Baby I think we have messages, should we get it?" "Let them wait, my wife comes first."

Todd continued to kiss Denise, but something told her that she needed to check the messages now. "Todd, baby I need to check the message." "Okay sweetheart go right ahead, and then you are all mine." "You got it!" Todd walked into the bathroom and Denise picked up the phone to retrieve the voice message. It was Todd's mother and Denise could barely understand what she was saying. All she could make out was her crying and screaming. Then Denise heard her say, "Please come home quick." The message had Denise so scared that she started crying and she didn't even know why. Todd heard Denise crying and ran out of the bathroom. "What is it, what's wrong?" "I don't know listen to this message, it's your mother." After Todd had listened to the message he started to panic as well. Denise grabbed their suitcases and started to throw things in them. Todd grabbed the phone to find out when the next flight out was. By the time they got to the airport they were both a bundle of nerves. They tried to call his mother several times. Then they tried to call Denise's mother and Freddy and couldn't get an answer anywhere.

The next day they arrived at Todd's mother's house. Todd hurried to open the door with his key. Once he got inside he started screaming, "Ma! Ma! Where are you?" "His mother walked down the steps and her face was swollen from crying and she grabbed Denise first and just held her. Denise looked at her and said, "Thank God you are okay. We were worried sick about you, what happened?" "Sit down baby." Denise sat down with her and took her hand. Todd held his mother's hand and said, "Ma you are scaring me. Don't worry whatever it is we will work it out. Did someone hurt you?" Denise looked at Todd's mother trying to figure out what was going on and asked her, "Please tell us, are you hurt?"

Todd's mother couldn't stop crying, Denise tried to console her. Todd was trying to console both of the women in his life and wait to hear what was wrong with his mother. Todd's mother looked at Denise and said, "It's not me baby, it's you." "What about me?" "It's your mother." "My mother…where is she? Is she hurt? What hospital is she in?" "She's with the Lord now, baby." Denise just looked at her in shock. She couldn't move she couldn't speak. Denise could hear Todd and his mother screaming and crying, but she couldn't move. Todd ran to Denise and grabbed her tight as she heard him say, "Denise baby I'm here for you, talk to me please." "She can't be dead. There is so much I need to tell her. I need to show her I can be the best nurse in Philly. Plus she has to manage our clinic. Who is going to manage it now?" (Denise started to break out into a deep cry that she couldn't control.)

Todd's mother looked like she was scared to death and said, "That's not all, sweetheart… I hate to tell you this but Freddy was with her. They were coming back from dinner the other night and got hit by a tractor trailer. They were in a big ten car pile up on the freeway. Three other people died in it too." Todd held Denise tight and they all started to cry as his mother put her arms around them both. Todd's mother started to pray and then Denise thought about Jeffrey and Jeanine. "My brother and sister, where are they? Lord please, not them too." "They're fine they have been staying with me. I didn't want them to be here when I told you, so Sister Gertrude from my church took them to a movie." "Do they know?" "Yes they know and we had our bereavement ministry counsel them and they seem to be dealing with it as well as to be expected.

Thank God they were with me when the accident happened. Nina asked me to watch them while her and Freddy went on a romantic dinner. I know this is going to be hard for all of us, they were good people. You must know that they are with the Lord now." "Yes I do. But why did he have to take them, why?" "We all get mad at the Lord sometimes because we don't understand why things are the way they are. Maybe we will never know. He has a plan and sometimes it is not for us to know." "I do know one thing…if I didn't have God right now I wouldn't be able to handle this."

It had been an extremely tough year for Denise trying to get past her mother's and Freddy's death. After Denise thought her and Todd couldn't get any closer, it was through their pain that they learned how to cherish each day together. Todd and Denise decided that Jeanine and Jeffrey would live with them. They bought a six bedroom house that was ten minutes away from his mother. They tried to get her to live with them several times, but she refused to leave her house. Todd's mother and Denise had become very close and she was just like a grandma to Jeanine and Jeffrey.

They found out after the funeral that Freddy had made up a will that left all his possessions to Nina and her kids. He had the will completed after they got married. Nina never had a will done. Denise figured maybe she thought she didn't have anything to leave them. But Denise felt like the transition she had made in her life, by becoming a wonderful and supporting mother to them was priceless. Since Todd and Denise were so young they thought it would be years before they would have to create a will. But when they realized that tomorrow is not promised to anyone they thought about their loved ones being taken care of. They wanted to make sure that Jeanine and Jeffrey would have a promising future.

So they went and had their wills made out. It made them both feel so much more secure, knowing that they had no worries if something were to happen. As Denise lounged on their porch she realized life was still good. She loved their home and her career. God had truly blessed their practice it had become very successful. Denise was slowly dealing with her mother's death and Freddy's death one day at a time. She was now serving on the bereavement board at their church and she started a woman's crisis center. Todd and Denise worked together in everything they did. Everything they touched was blessed and she knew that she was fulfilling her purpose here on earth. Even though her mother was taken away from her, it was her faith in God that kept her sanity. Now Denise was able to use that same faith and trust to counsel other women that were carrying the load of loosing a loved one.

Todd walked up behind Denise and put his arms around her as she looked out into the yard watching Jeanine and Jeffrey play catch. As Todd playfully patted her stomach he said, "Dag baby you gaining a little weight but you wear it well." "That's what happens when you plant a seed." "What seed?" "Your seed baby, I'm pregnant." "Bless the Lord!" Todd hugged and kissed Denise so tight that she couldn't move. Then the twins ran over and said, "Would you love birds cut it out." "Your sister is having a baby. I mean we're having a baby!" Todd ran out into the yard shouting to the neighbors, "We're having a baby, bless the Lord! Bless the Lord!" As the twins ran up to Denise, Todd ran back up on the porch behind them. They all rushed up to Denise and hugged and kissed her and at that very moment she knew she had found a little peace of heaven, right here on earth.

About the Author

After giving her life to Christ and experiencing God's love, the author wrote this short inspirational story to encourage someone else who might be going through a difficult time. This powerful story is about overcoming the pain and hurt of tragedy that can overtake your life, the choices that we make to contribute to our failures, and the power within us to overcome them.

Printed in the United States
24680LVS00003B/140

9 781420 809923